The Sniper

Anthony V. La Penta, Jr.

ISBN: 1469902893
ISBN-13: 9781469902890

Library of congress Control Number: 2012900744
CreateSpace, North Charleston, SC

Dedicated to the three most important women in my life,
Natalie, Catherine and Alice.

Acknowledgments

Thanks to my father Anthony, and grandfather Francisco.

Thanks and appreciation go to the following experts that aided me with technical knowledge in the preparation of this book:

James Tremont – for his technical advice on ballistics

Ed Morin, Danny Winter and Leo Souza – Firemen, Hayden Station Fire Department, Windsor, Connecticut

Capt. Frank A. LaPenta, Capt. Joseph Biernacki and former Sergeant Glenn P. McCarthy, Jr., United States Army, for their expertise on Vietnam and Airborne School

Officers Jerry Martin, of the Hartford Police Department and Steven Cudworth of the Canton Police Department

Many thanks also go to the people who gave me support in going through my first drafts,
Susie Havel, Nicole Putnam and Christopher LaPenta.

Foreword

Sniper, by definition, is an expert marksman, who can consistently hit with his first shot, a target as small as a man's head, at distances up to and over three hundred yards, under varying conditions of light and weather (circa 1970). Depending on weapon and cartridge, targets can now be attained at between one thousand and two thousand meters (today).

"And no one is angry enough to speak out."
Inscribed on an ancient Egyptian tomb.

CHAPTER ONE

1970 AD

It had been a busy, chaotic Friday night. Even more so tonight, it's "shopping night" at the grocery store. It seems like the whole town stops to go shopping on Fridays. People, winding their way in and out of the electric doors, looking like gaily decorated lines of ribbons, strewn about. Carts scattered where cars should have been. Cars were where carts belonged. Even the endless stars shining through the smog seemed to add to the confusion.

Within the store, the faced off stacked displays of food waited like soldiers to be picked off. Children were running and screaming in and out of aisles, caroming off people. Husbands were bringing up the rear, pushing carts laden with food, while the wives became scouts, trying to find the necessary commodities for future meals. People were hurrying here and there, when there was no real need to. Disorder was everywhere.

The voices in the store forced together to keep a subtle humming of motors and vehicle rumbling in a parking lot. Individually the chaos was maintained within each conversation as you walked through.

"Dear, you missed the sugar. Hold the kids and the cart and I'll go get it."

"Oh no! No, you don't. Nice try. You keep the cart and the monsters; *I'll* go get the sugar."

A little boy dressed in an army jacket and helmet carrying a bayonet and M-16, charging his imaginary enemy through the aisles, inevitably collided with the shoppers. This time, it was him.

"Hey, watch it soldier! You keep running like that and they'll get you." The man picked up the fallen weapon and looked it over fondly.

"That's a nice looking weapon, boy. Not quite like the one I had, but it'll do ... it'll do ... "

"It'll do for a soldier, don't worry. This rifle is like a part of me, and anything that gets in front of it can kiss off life."

The two men sat there clutching their weapons and quickly glancing and looking over their shoulders in all directions. Somehow through the state of alertness, they maintained a normal conversation, purely a display of the human ability to adapt to new and adverse situations.

"I suppose, but this 16's a lot faster than your Garand. The only thing you've got working for you is that scope and silencer ... that might give you an edge."

"Might my ass. You know I have an edge."

"Yeah, well edge or no edge, I wish this damn patrol was over and we could get back. The weather's too damn hot, the ground's dirty, the women are cold. Just staying on edge, expecting, looking, waiting. Don't know who's going to try and give it to you."

The older man somewhat sighed. It was the story of everyone's life these days. Nothing you could do about it.

"I don't like it any more than you do, friend. I don't like this land, the people or anything else here. It's not my war. When those people at home say we're fighting for a reason, it's true – we sure as hell are, and that reason is survival. Out here, you don't worry about anything but your own ass, your people. If you got time, I wouldn't mind some cover. The more of us that stay alive, the better our chance for survival."

He forced a smile. It was all too real to be that happy. He knew that wouldn't be enough to satisfy the other soldier. He was already shaking his head before he spoke. There really was nothing to be said that would calm his nerves or make him feel good, short of getting everyone home.

"That sounds alright on the surface, but you don't believe that we're here to stop the reds, that because the more of a hold they get on anybody's land the more of a threat they are to our great democracy? All they are doing is waiting for the right time, then they'll clobber us. You've got it made ... "

He continued talking but the sniper knew where he was going. Everyone always thinks about it a day late and a dollar short – why didn't I become a sniper? Truth was, you didn't because you couldn't. Sorry sonny, that's just the way it is. It's what we're dealt, and we all have to play it.

" ... If you don't like the killing and all, and you're just out here trying to survive, how did you end up as a sniper of the platoon, and everyone knows you as the kill shot? Survive ... "

"You're right, and because you're so pretty and dumb, I'll explain it. I hate killing with a passion even I don't quite understand."

He could feel his mood changing, growing more intense and subtle as he spoke. His eyes began to glaze over and though he would never recognize it in himself, he was mentally preparing to take a shot.

"But I also realize this is a war where people do get killed. When you're hit, and blood starts coming out of that little temple of flesh of yours, you get mighty worried and scared. You start to understand that if you die out here, you're dead. It's not like T.V. where you get up after the take or a bad dream and your mom is coming to hold you. Ain't nobody dying but you. I used to hate cowards. When I was little, I thought no true American likes cowards. Now, I know I don't want to die, and son of a bitch, most cowards are alive and well."

"What's that got to do with over here? Those guys call you mean and ruthless, but coward? Un uh ... " Pearls before swine. It's easier just to shoot them.

"Listen! Just keep your head out of your ass, breathe fresh air so your mind can work. If I don't kill people, in the eyes of all those people, I am a coward. But I do it to survive. I'm here. And nothing I do or say is going to change that. *I* didn't volunteer to fight. I was drafted. I'm making the best of a fucking lousy situation. War is war, and since I'm here in this *beautiful* country, if any person attempts to hurt my body, I will personally and thoroughly kill the son of a bitch dead, be it man, woman or child. I wanted the Sniper shot, because a sniper works alone. I rely only on myself and I only have myself to watch out for, I don't need to watch out for a group of scared kids who are gonna get me fucking blown away."

They both sat silent. He realized that sometimes honesty is not the best answer. He just put all his bullshit on the table for a kid who was talking to him so he could feel better. Now he knows he's going to die out here, and nobody, not even the hero sniper, is going to save him. Way to go hoss, way to go.

"I read a poem once ... " His voice was softer, no less of a killer, but somehow compassionate, even for those people that would fall before him. " ... and it stuck with me, and now I guess, I like it even more."

The younger soldier looked up at him from the ground, with the humility of death still fresh on his mind, he pulled closer to the snipers feet, and for a brief moment in time, two people could have been mistaken for teacher and pupil, or father and son, maybe even friends.

"War is a God damned thing!
It is foolish.
It is for the little children,
Who do not know how to solve an argument.

It is not heroic or beauty,
Rather it is filthy and miserable.
War takes away man's most wonderful gift: life.
Men hate, boys kill, life is wasted.
The youth of the world is taken
and destroyed.
War is quicksand that engulfs all.

Some think war has rules.
God damn it, wake up!
War is war. There are no rules.
It's kill or be killed.
It takes no valor to kill men,
Only self-protection.
War is the ruthless battle for survival.

Mercy is a foreign word.
Fear Fear Fear!
It comes and gnaws at the body,
As worms to the corpse.
It is not for the purpose of saving a life,

But taking it.
War is hell on earth.

Darkness for those that seek light,
Silence for the men that speak
Mist and fog for the unknown land,
All for the ignorance that brought it life
War is the eternal light,
Dim and forever."

The mood was no less morbid, but less personalized. For the time being it was someone else's words on war ringing in their ears. That was all the sniper wanted. The soldier couldn't help but pull himself back into it, his egotism would be his downfall, killing from a distance is the only way to really survive.

"That's not too bad. I kinda agree with the guy. In a way it sort of explains your gun – oh, oh, pardon me – your rifle."

"Rifle is right, friend, and in a way like this one, if you want to survive, you've gotta have good equipment. With this rifle, which I have personally equipped with my own silencer, and adjusted sight, I figure I have just about the best equipment around. And like I said, being a sniper, I only have to worry about myself. It's lonely but it beats pounding the grass with 12 other guys that might get distracted or make a mistake."

He held his rifle close as he talked, looking it over and caressing it, knowing how it has kept him alive until now, and would keep him going until he got home. He could tell the other soldier was watching him, not really understanding the bond between the man and his weapon. A sound.

"What's that?"

The sniper spoke quietly to himself, heart already beginning to beat faster, and body already melting to the earth.

"What's what?"

"Shut up! Drop. *Now.*"

Both men fell to the ground, rolled over several times in an effort to find better cover, ending near a heavy clump of bushes.

"Goddamn dirty bushes ... "

"For Christ's sake – shut your ... "

"Watch out behind you!"

As he aimed his weapon, I turned and tried to fire, but the bush blocked my view. He had his gun ready and set to automatic. The man seemed to disintegrate, bits of skin and blood flying all over. Just as his limp body dropped to the ground, two more were on us. My rifle was kicked from my hands, and this man, this stranger, was trying to kill me. There was a hot flash in my leg as I diverted his aim, and then this little bastard was on top of me. I tried to knee his groin at the same time I reached to tear his ears. His hands were choking me and making their way to my eyes.

With one hand I tried to get my knife, but the damn thing was stuck in the scabbard. With a heave I threw him off me and ripped the knife, scabbard and all right off my web belt. He lunged forward and I thrust out with all my force; the combined power pushed the whole damn thing right into his throat. I jerked and the knife finally came free. He looked at me with so much surprise, put his hands to his throat and pulled out the sheath. His eyes started to roll back and he fell to the ground, but not before drenching me with blood.

I turned. I could see the guerilla on top of the soldier, a rock in his hand, poised – read to strike. My rifle was too far away. Everything moved in slow motion. His eyes and face contorted as he struggled futilely to free himself. A scream filled my head, almost forcing my eyes to close. The guerilla brought the rock down ever so slowly; there was a dull crack and then a thud. I jumped on the boy's back and wrapped my left arm around his neck. My other hand still held my virgin knife. With a strength born in battle, I brought my knife to his back. I was surprised at the thickness of the clothes, but there was little resistance as the blade punctured the skin. I felt the grate of the bone as I hit the spinal column. He moaned and fell lifelessly.

I stood and looked at yet another "unsung hero", gently removed his dog tags, and any personal items he may have wanted returned to family at home. As I picked up my rifle, a wounded guerilla moaned. I turned around to find he was still alive. I didn't have much choice and at that moment in all honesty, I didn't care that much. I was too weak to carry him as a P.O.W. and with a wound like he had, he wouldn't survive anyway. I fed a 308 into my rifle and pulled the trigger. For the moment – silence. I walked away.

"Hey mister! Can I have my gun back? Huh? I gotta go find my mom."

"Uh! Oh, sure sonny."

The man rubbed the little boys head as he smiled down at him.

"Just got lost in thought for a moment. I had better get going myself, Princess might get worried."

CHAPTER TWO

The day we met – like the time worn story of boy meets girl. We might as well have been actors in a movie. Some days everything just works out right. Whether it's the moon and the sun that align or the gods decide to smile upon you, sometimes life feels like it should.

I was on leave, taking the bus home. Who happens to be on the bus but a cute girl sitting by herself. I will remember how helplessly cute, like some kid out on their own for the first time. She was loaded with bags and sort of stumbled and swayed with the motion of the bus. I thought I'd play the gentleman role and offer my seat, maybe an easy in to get to know her. As I stood up, the bus made a hard lurch forward, and I felt my foot get tangled in my duffel bag. I tried to brace myself but the titanic had a better chance of staying up. I fell right into the girl, knocking her packages all over the floor of the bus, and then for good measure, hit my chin on the seat next to mine. I had just dragged myself to my feet, preparing to apologize profusely when the bus decided to stop short. The girl who just finished picking up her packages and straightening up, landed in my arms.

"Whoa! I'm the one who's supposed to make the passes, not you."

She turned a crimson sort of color, which she would continue to do every time I would ever say anything that would embarrass her.

"I didn't mean anything of the kind and ... oh, you're hurt."

She reached up and gently touched my chin.

"It isn't anything that several days of intensive care and a 24 hour heart monitor wouldn't cure. Really, it's just a cut on my chin. It served me right, I guess, for trying to play the "knight in shining armor" bit. I should have looked where I was going."

"That's true, but I do feel somewhat responsible for your hurting yourself."

I knew we were already into each other. She was genuine and concerned for my well-being, as well as interested in this less than gracious knight. And I was more and more attracted to her and loved how she handled herself.

"Tell you what, you say you feel responsible, have the guilty conscience, gonna throw yourself over the next bridge we drive past ... well I have another suggestion. Since I just got in town – and the only people I know in the whole town are my parents, who just moved here. How about I take you out to dinner tonight?"

I could tell I was winning her over so I kept going.

"You know, wine and dine you, no funny stuff. Seriously, I just feel like going out and celebrating. I've got my pay from overseas and want to spend some of it – give the sagging economy a boost. O.K.?"

"Well, I don't know. I don't even know you. You're a *complete* stranger."

"Well you said you wanted to make it up to me, that you felt guilty ... "

She was smiling, enjoying my playfulness.

"I never said ... "

" ... and since you want to do something to get my mind off the pain and reward my good intentions, come to dinner with me. It will make me happy. Besides, you look like you could spot a wolf a mile away. Honestly, do I look like one to you?"

I motioned to the area of the accident and then smiled baring all my teeth.

"Well, no, you look more like a spastic ... alright, I'll take a chance."

"Great. Where do you live?"

I noticed I was just staring at her and watching her mouth move as she talked. I could hear the words but it wasn't sinking in. I had too many happy thoughts running through my head.

"Did you ever consider being a pathfinder?"

She smiled that big smile again.

"It's not that hard. Do you know where the Fire Station is? I live in the third white house on the right once you've passed it."

"I'll be there at eight? If that's good for you?"

It's funny how you know the answer to a question but you can still get the nervous butterflies. It's like the final piece brings you full circle, back to your original feelings maybe.

"Yes, that would be fine. What should I wear?"

"I hear clothes are really in this year ... "

I didn't wait for her to say "very funny" but just kept it going.

" ... wear something cool. We are going to flip this town over tonight."

I smiled. And glanced out the windows at the passing houses, getting my bearings on where I was. We had been talking for a while and I wasn't paying attention to anything but her and that smile.

"Right now I'm going to get off this bus, because I passed my stop about six blocks ago, but I'll see you tonight at eight."

"But I don't even know your name."

One last chance to say something smart or charming. My final page to the first chapter in what would be the book of our lives.

Sometimes everything comes together, and you can always look back at it and smile.

I looked back from the door of the bus, hand still on the rail as the door opened. "Call me your shining knight, and you'll be my princess. See you at eight."

I got there around eight and waited until it was seven fifty-nine before I started the walk from the car to the door. She lived in a nice little house, painted white with green shutters. There was a brand new aluminum door with the capital "S" in a circle in the middle. I wondered what her last name was. Princess S. I rang the bell, smoothed my hair and made sure the polish particles were off my shoes. I always wipe the shoes clean, and I always remembered why.

I once had a date with a girl I really liked, so I not only shaved, showered and wore a shirt and tie, I went the extra mile and put two coats of polish on my shoes. Unfortunately, it was raining that night and I didn't have a car. By the time I reached her house I was soaked. As I was meeting her parents, standing there, shaking hands and answering the usual questions, the polish on my shoes, both coats of that black polish, were dripping down the sides of my shoes onto their gold carpet. Looking back, I should have said that I not only made an impression on their daughter but it looks like I left my mark on their floor as well. I laughed out loud to myself just as the door opened.

There was Princess. A short light pink dress hugged her body and a single strand of pearls around her throat. I felt that feeling again – the feeling like everything is the way it should be, and life really is a beautiful thing and we are lucky to have it. I stared again, this time for too long and she began to worry something was wrong.

"What? ... Is my lipstick smudged? ... "

I moved slightly closer to her and took her hand. I could have kissed her then, but I wanted to tell her how good she looked. I wanted her to know, she was the most beautiful sight I had ever seen.

"You look ... fantastic."

I spoke slowly and sincerely, and I'm sure my eyes wandered all over her body and back again. Her smile returned and she motioned for me to come in with her.

"Thank you, kind knight. Won't you step inside and meet my parents?"

Five minutes later, I was closing the door behind us, excited to get the night underway. I hadn't ruined anyone's carpet ... so far I was feeling pretty good about my performance.

"That was painless."

She was walking toward the car in front of me, still looking beautiful. Carefree. I realized that I hadn't been here in some time, and I never was a big socialite, so I had no idea where we could go to eat, never mind something that would be nice enough for how she was dressed.

I smiled. "Things have no doubt changed so much since I was last here, where do you recommend we eat? Remembering that I am the last of the big spenders, and am ready to go as high as two dollars apiece for the night's festivities?"

"Oh! What a *nice* car."

I let her look it over for a minute before I told her it belonged to my parents.

"It's my dad's."

"I bet they were glad to see you home, safe and sound."

She was no doubt thinking there may have been some bad blood between us. It wasn't uncommon. A lot of people had stories and tears for fights that should never have happened and never had a chance to get resolved. This was a fun night, though. And I was one of the lucky ones."

"Yeah, I guess he lost the bet they had going. I cost him 5 bucks by making it back in one piece."

She smiled and swatted my arm. She was right, I was a kidder. It felt good to be so light.

"No, they were both very happy. My old man actually cried a little. My father always said there was nothing wrong with a man showing a little emotion now and then, but that was the first time I ever saw him cry. I guess he's sort of a romantic."

She was circling the car as I talked, still smiling as she spoke.

"Your father sounds nice."

She stopped walking and looked directly at me and the smile was all mine.

"I know where we can go, c'mon. It's right up the street, in downtown."

She was right. It was a nice place right up the street. Subdued lighting, flickering candles, clinking of glasses and silverware, people talking almost in whispers, all added a very romantic and elegant atmosphere – one in which she blended perfectly as the centerpiece.

"This certainly is nice. The food is excellent; the ambiance is exactly what I was looking for. Makes up for all the army chow and mess halls."

"You looked like you were putting every piece up for "analyzation" before you ate it."

I stopped and held the piece of meat on my fork over my plate, and realized she was truly right. I was looking it over as we spoke. For a moment I wondered if I was forever changed or if it was something that could be forgotten. I'm sure she heard the slight worry in my voice, and prepared to calm me with her positive perspective, like she would always do.

"Is it that obvious? Does it show that I have been away that much?"

"No, not really." She said nonchalantly. "You just look like a man savoring his meal." She bit the meat off of her fork as she finished her sentence and smiled at me more playfully, and I was sold. She could have told me I looked like the President and I would have run with it. Still, I chose to explain my appreciation ... I knew she was smart enough to appreciate it.

"You know, here, stateside, everything is so clean. Really, people talk about litter and dumps, but when you're in a jungle for a year, and you have dirt in your clothes and dirt in your food and dirt in your water and everything is this green-brown world, and then all of a sudden you come back to this place, where there isn't even dirt on the ground and you have all these bright colors and everything is clean ... You wear your clothes, ya know. You don't use them for napkins, handkerchief, dust rag, and all-purpose wipe."

The chatter of the restaurant continues and the sniper's rant blends in, never rising above the expected decibel level, maybe even softening. They are fading out from him though, and he is losing sight of what is before him but remembering the greens and browns that constituted his life for so long. Her pink dress even becomes dulled down as he continues to speak. Finally he looks up and sees her not eating, but holding her fork looking at him with compassion but no real understanding.

"Princess, you don't want to know what it's like to live like an animal. Thinking about home and country and the people back home doesn't mean a whole hell of a lot. I don't know. You'd think that God gave us a mind to reason, and I've always heard that all men are brothers. Apparently this great gift of reason is better spent on getting a man to the moon. You are only brothers with people that you don't covet their wealth, land or power ... "

The sniper realizes he is off target. He is in the wrong place and time for this conversation, and he knows it. The color slowly beings to come back to her dress and the sound fades back from the jungle noise and gunfire to the clattering silverware, wine glasses and happy banter.

"I'm sorry."

He shook it off, but never let me down, or left me on my own.

"My, you do get carried away on certain things, don't you? At least on things you care about, things you believe in, things you've risked your life for. I don't blame you, for feeling angry or mad at the people that make wars, and I don't blame you for having the strength to fight them."

She was right and she knew it. There was nothing he could do about it, but he couldn't stop the feeling that someone should do something about it. It wasn't fair and it wasn't right.

"Not much point in complaining about it here and now, is there though? Not like I can do anything about how the world works, or the wars that get fought. No point in worrying over things you can't change. I just feel like blaming somebody. I know it won't make it go away or change anything." I kind of chuckle to myself as I feel my own pointless struggle. "I don't even think it would make me feel any better. I just think the people, the smart ones, the ones that lead the followers by the nose. I can blame the dumb ones for following in the first place. Why would you be so trusting?"

Princess had a way of keeping things cool and legitimate. This wasn't a pointless rage of an ex-army man, but a political discussion between two very civilized and intelligent individuals.

"It sounds as if your faith is with the people, and it is the leaders that you feel have let down their country, and led them astray. A lot of people would agree with you. In fact, I think that may be one of the very premises of democracy. Although I wish they would act more independently than along party lines, as they do."

With articulation like that, the conversation was not only in its place in the restaurant, but probably the most appropriate one. She kept eating and smiling occasionally and I maintained a level of composure as I continued to take in all of my surroundings. So many people enjoying themselves in such a nice place.

"I think in time, people will no longer be led by these so called leaders but they will truly have a voice in their own destiny. They will actually be helped by the leaders, then it will be really run by the people. The only time we would go to war, is when the majority of the country, all its people, truly wanted to and thought it was in the best interest. Not one person, not big business ... the people."

She already seemed accustomed to his talking. She continued to eat, unhindered by his choice of conversation or his passion on the subject. It was a great night, and she seemed to have known that from the beginning. He was focusing on it right now.

"Here I am talking, and this fantastic night, with a *real* girl, is going by right before my eyes. C'mon, let's dance."

He stood and extended his hand as she sipped her glass of wine and then put it down to the table. They walked over to the wooden floor hand in hand and began to dance.

"You dance well and look beautiful."

"Thank you, kind sir. You've got a little dance in you too."

"Hey, I've got an idea. Let's go out and ride around in that nice car of mine, and just be you and me."

"O.K., but remember, no funny stuff." She said it entirely for the humor; she had no doubt in the world that the man she was with was all gentleman.

"I promise you will not see anything funny for the rest of the night."

We made our way to the car, after I left a better than decent tip and this time I chose the destination. The road was empty and the night was dark except for the two beams of light shining from the Chevy. The car wound its way to the top of the hill just outside of town. Beneath it, the houses and streets lay still and the stars twinkling.

"It's very nice here, quiet and soft ... you can see the wind just skimming across the trees. Princess, I'm very happy I met you, and if you'll pardon my bluntness, I like you very much."

She smiled sincerely at me and then returned her gaze back out at the sleeping town.

CHAPTER THREE

"Hey honey, I'm home. What's for supper? The grocery store was swamped."

He hung his coat on the rack and was making his way to the kitchen of a very modest apartment to see her, but she leaned back from the stove in the doorway and beat him to it.

"Your favorite. How did it go – any good prospects today or should we not wait by the phone?"

He rubbed her back as she opened the refrigerator and grabbed the orange juice. He looked solemnly at the glass briefly before pouring.

"Are you kidding? The places are locked up tighter than drums. No one seems to want a fairly intelligent fellow with two years of college experience."

She may have sighed but it never showed. She kept right on cooking and being lighthearted in the conversation.

"You have to have a degree and related experience before these people even look at you. Which is a pretty dumb and vicious circle ... you can't very well get related experience if you need experience to get hired, now can you?"

He drank from his glass as she turned to smile.

"And you only said you were fairly intelligent."

"The only real experience I have is with a rifle, and I'm damn good with it. I'd love to see any of these pencil pushers get my experience. Then they would know what it's like to earn something and work hard. I guarantee I'd do a lot better at their job than they would at mine."

The cooking never stopped, but her tone was audibly changed. She sounded concerned, leery of a fight, but thought it was necessary to mention.

"Speaking of army and guns and all that jazz, I meant to ask you about taking down that gun out of the den and putting it away somewhere. You know how nervous it makes me."

He looked at his princess, finished his juice, and shrugged his shoulders.

"Yeah, but no matter how nervous it makes you, that gun is the thing that brought us together. Do you know that a 308 at 18 hundred yards is just as powerful as a .45 at point blank range?"

Now she sighed visibly.

"Yes dear. You've told me that one *hundred* times, at least."

He knew she was right. He did talk about his gun – his rifle – a lot. Why shouldn't he? He had a half a mind to say what he never told her about when he was in airborne. When he had guns so much on his mind he came up with modifications to weapons to make them more efficient at killing. He looked his princess over and saw the spinach start to boil over as she tended the meat. She had enough going on and he probably did talk about it too much. Just because he can't stop thinking about it didn't mean he had to always share. He poured himself another glass of orange juice and kept his memories to himself.

"Love this Airborne, Sarge, it's a real body builder."

A young man, in good shape with a helmet marked "43" stood anxiously at the edge. The older man, seeing his confidence as real as youth may have, spoke without concern.

"Never mind sonny, just get that harness on and get ready to jump."

The men stood in a tower that was over thirty feet tall, with facsimile airplane doors. A second tower stood at 250 feet just off to the side, just close enough so you could see what you were getting into. The first jump was the hardest, even though it wasn't nearly as high, just because it was the first. There were wires attached to the backpack of the jumper, and if you didn't hold your neck and head down when jumping, you could get a pretty good lash from them as they shot out as they were being deployed. The first week of training consisted entirely of body training, getting all these young men prepared for the shock and pain of enduring jumping dozens and eventually hundreds of feet through the air.

The drill sergeants made it all the happier with yes sir, no sir, yes drill sergeant, no drill sergeant; 10, 20, 30 sit ups, squat thrusts, push ups and then bend, run, ache, sleep, swear, sweat. Through it all, everyone had to wonder if they could even make it, and eventually if they even wanted to. The second week, when the actual jump-training started, it was as if things had improved a little.

"Well 43, you going to jump or not? Just step and go."

He stepped out into space and fell. Surprised at how fast the less than 2 second drop really was, he felt the harness catch and bounced a little as he hit – forgetting the nervousness in his stomach when he was standing at the top looking down.

The third week was when we faced the final test – five jumps from a height of 1,250 feet. Although it's not as high as you would make a real jump, it's high enough to make quite a splash if something goes wrong. Usually nothing does. Once I got over the fear of splashing, and forgot I was about to jump out of a plane, it was quite beautiful. The green fields and brown earth, all the trees with different color leaves. It was amazing to think that this was reserved only for people jumping out of a plane in wartime, usually in the thick of the fight.

It was an amazing feeling, even through the fear. After the initial jump, when you're out there going down, it's almost like you don't want the chute to open. But then when it does, that's a whole other feeling of floating, soaring through the sky, as the straps pull at you.

My third time in the plane – ready to go – and one of the guys ahead of me froze.

"Number 23! JUMP!"

"Yes SIR!"

He was still poised at the door, looking down, and trembling. His hands and face were getting more pale as he stood ready.

"Jump or get out of the way, 23. Do something!"

"I can do this sir ... I'm trying."

"Unhook and come back, 23. This is not the time to try."

There was no animosity in his order. I imagined he had seen this dozens of times. It was 23's first time, not his. The young soldier unhooked his clip as he turned to come back out of the door – as the plane hit an air pocket rocking it. He should have just jumped. Now his face was fixed with terror as he reached desperately for anything to hold him inside the plane. His mouth opened to scream, what we were all feeling, but he fell silently out of the plane. Without a sound he was gone, his clip swinging on the line.

The man's yelling, "Open your chute, open your chute!!!" was futile, he would not hear him, and I wasn't sure that he would have remained calm enough to do it, especially now. We came down after that and later we heard that they recovered his body, auxiliary chute unopened. I never even knew his name. I don't think anyone really did. Number 23.

It's probably better that I don't remember everything out loud.

"You know, dear, that's the trouble with the world today."

She was still stirring and cooking the food.

"What's the trouble with the world today, what are you talking about?"

"To strangers, you're faceless, you're nameless. It's like we might as well have numbers on our heads like the army does .... .or a computer card at school. When you go to a job, except for the few friends you make along the way, you're more or less a statistic, a social security number on a payroll or whatever. Everyone knows that you exist, sure. As a name, attached to a serial number and date of birth; they are just symbols all tied together without any real connection to each person."

This conversation had become more prevalent, but she was able to adapt quickly and learn how to keep it under wraps. She began setting the table as she spoke quietly, appreciating his feeling but trying to enforce that it isn't all bad.

"That's true, dear. But, I think it's not that people don't want to get to know people, it's just hard to get to know everyone these days. The numbers for everything is going up, even people. It would be very difficult to get to know even half the people you come in contact with throughout the day."

He sighed and came back out of the plane fully and into his kitchen, where his princess did know him and he knew her. Together they lived in their quaint little place and cared for each other. He grabbed her as he was walking by for more silverware and pulled her onto his lap. Looking up into her eyes smiling.

"I just think everyone needs at least one person. Someone that knows you lived and died."

"Right! And now that dinner is ready, here is one time that a person, namely myself, has cooked it so that another person, namely you, can eat it, thus completing a circle of appreciation for a person. Got it?"

She was smiling broadly now and was back on her feet preparing to serve the food. He smiled to her back and followed her lead.

"Yes, my love --- boy, you are an ass."

"Oh I like that, such talk."

"I'm sort of partial to it myself."

"Very funny number 31341362. Just eat."

She put a plate down in front of him, and once again he couldn't help but think how she had taken inexpensive ingredients and served a gourmet meal. When they were done eating and he had his fill, he expressed gratitude in the normal smile and kiss.

"Excellent meal, princess. Now if I could only find a job this would be something."

"Don't worry so much about it. We're getting along just fine on my salary and something will come along soon."

"I know we're getting along, but I want to work; that's *my* job ... to support us – not yours. And it's going to be pretty hard to start a family, if you know what I mean."

He motioned to his belly and stuck it out as far as he could. She knew she had a point, but there was no point in fretting now, and besides they weren't doing that bad financially. She looked at him in anticipation for what was really on his mind and his face lost its humor, as he half turned out the window.

"Do your parents know I'm still out of work?"

"Yes, they do. And they wish I wouldn't work so hard, and they wish that you could find a job, and probably that there was peace on earth."

"What the hell do they think I'm doing? Do they *really* think I like sitting around the house, cleaning and running errands? Losing my masculinity more every day. Yeah, that's just the bullshit I signed up for when I got out of the war. I figured I had enough mans' stuff for a while. I know they care about you, but it's not like I don't. Somehow I always feel like they think I'm mistreating you or I have more power over the situation than I really do, and that I'm just loafing around being a lazy ass."

"Alright, everyone knows you love me, and you are trying to find a job. Stop worrying what they think so much anyway. And you look so cute in an apron, I don't mind at all."

Her usual light heart wasn't winning him over as easily these days; the bills piling up, the thought of being a failure, the memories of war, everything seemed to outweigh her, and she wasn't winning these battles as much.

"Damn it, I'm serious. Sometimes they really do piss me off. I know they are talking about me, probably right now. 'He's no good; I knew she should have never married him; probably just sits around drinking all day,' and who knows what other shit they say."

He was visibly irritated and it seemed that he grew more and more out of touch lately when he had these moments. She was never fearful, but always remembered what he had been through.

"Well, maybe they are just worried about us. My asthma has been getting worse. The other day I had an attack with my mom ... "

"I know it's getting worse. Obviously I know. There are bills to pay, so you work hard, you get sick and then there are more bills to pay, so you have to work harder – it doesn't take Einstein to figure this shit out. Goddamn thing just goes round and round and gets worse as it goes. EVERYBODY'S worried. Not just them. You're worried, I'm worried, the doc is worried."

"Well, I'm sorry I get sick and have to stop work sometimes, but once you get a job it won't matter and then I can take a day off without even being sick for a change."

"I'm trying, damn it. I don't have a college degree, and to get anything these days you need that stupid little piece of paper."

"You're using that as an excuse for an awful lot lately. I wish you'd get off that line. If you don't want to take a job because you think you're too good for it, fine. Just stop making excuses."

"O.K., O.K., just stop yelling. You're starting to cough, and you know the doctor said try not to upset yourself. Christ, I feel bad enough about you working, and not being able to find a job, but when you start coughing like that ... "

The change from laughter to irritation to argument had been subtle and worked itself in and knotted with each one of them in its own way. Anger for one, and self-pity for another. The two had no idea that being so close and passionate could end with such pain. It was as though all their frustrations could only be vented on each other, spewing like garbage from a sewer in the polluted streets below. It would continue until it was through venting, and the anger that wasn't with each other, but with circumstances beyond anyone's control, was released.

"You are just scared. You can't face the world for what it is. You'd rather complain about how it's unfair just because people don't bend over backwards for you. Well why should they, huh? What the hell makes you so special? Just grow up."

"I fought and survived a world and horrors you can't even imagine. You don't have a goddamned clue what scared means. And I'll tell you what makes me so damn special ... "

"You aren't really that special. It was a rhetorical question. You don't deserve special treatment; you don't deserve anything you don't earn. And you can't keep living off that stupid gun in the living room."

Both people were visibly agitated, breathing hard and looking exhausted. These fights were only getting worse and lasting longer.

I couldn't believe my ears. It was like she had finally put her cards on the table, and I was all in, and never saw it coming. It was a stupid gun. And I wasn't special. If I hadn't hit so many people to kill them I swear I would have hit her then. Instead I ended up grabbing her by the throat and backing her up against the wall. Waving my finger in her face ranting the whole while in a voice I don't think she has ever heard. When I was done yelling, I let her go and turned around to grab my coat and saw her kneeling on the ground where she had fallen, as I slammed the door behind me.

When I was a kid, if I got angry, I would just walk outside. Walking the streets for a while would cool me off not matter how old I got, I guess. I started to feel better right away, but what she said hurt. You don't say that kind of thing unless you mean it, and how could she have meant it all this time and never told me? My mind didn't want to think all of these questions nor their answers.

Was it raining? My face was wet. I choked her. My god. I treated her like an enemy. I reverted to being an animal and attacked the only one in the world who really loved me in spite of everything I am. Jesus, other people cause me trouble, other people cause the problems, and I take it out on her. Hurt her. Maybe I *am* scared.

I walked into a bar, looked immediately for a seat close to the tender and sat down. It was noisy and hot, and the smoke lingered like it owned the place. I began looking around at all the anonymous faces. All the people. It was like I was accusing them and they were answering me, all the while without speaking.

"Who, me? I never did anything to you. I'm just living my own life, trying to take care of my own business."

"That's where you are guilty, friend. That's the trouble I'm speaking about. Your plea was really an admission of guilt. Everyone only takes care of their own and that's their excuse to let everything else ride and that's why everything is the way it is. That's why I spent two years killing people I never met, all the way to why Princess has asthma from a polluted city."

It's strange that we live for 70 years, and can't seem to spare one minute of feeling for anyone else. I guess I'm that way too. I may not see it, but I'm just the same. Maybe I have to be like everyone else just to get by. Like a car on the highway, the speed posted Is 40 mph, but you'll get run right off the road if you try to stick to it. Everyone is going at least 50. To survive, a comparable speed must be maintained. I *have* to drive 50, no matter who gets hurt or how much I want to drive 40.

"You want another drink?"

"Uh? Oh, yeah. Make it the same."

"Right."

The bartender walked away to the other end of the bar and revealed my mirror reflection. Boy, I look intelligent. Sad eyed, wet, and now drunk. What am I doing here? Feeling sorry for myself. Your wife is hurting, and you're nursing a drink. Go back, talk to her. Better yet, pack your things and leave. Go somewhere and get a job. Go back to where 40 is still the norm. There will probably be lots of jobs and living space for growing families there too. That way you can live like you always talked about ... I threw some money down and walked out. This was going to be the one thing I do right.

The rain was beautiful, the night was soft and embracing all in her darkness – as though the darkness were the light and everything was beautifully lit. I was alive. I could feel every breath I took. I had my health, my princess who loved me, and we were going to leave this dirty place. We would really make it. I was happy and had everything that mattered. I started to run home, not caring if people started. I didn't stop until I had gone up the stairs to our door, and then it was only for a moment to catch my breath before yelling to my wife.

"Honey, everything is going to be alright. You are right. I am scared, but I think ..."

I stopped in my tracks as I saw her slumped over in the same spot I left her in the kitchen. There was a puddle of blood by her mouth and she looked pale and lifeless. I ran over and grabbed her.

"My god Jesus no, No No No No NO! Honey! Princess, speak to me baby!"

He is frantic as he speaks to her, holding her head up and tapping her cheek, hoping she will regain consciousness. Nothing. She had been gone for too long.

What had happened? This can't be happening. I was going to tell her that it was all going to be alright. That she was right. That I was sorry.

He stayed there – sitting by her with her head in his arms on his lap, crying. The night went by and the next day began. He wouldn't remember much. There were alternate periods of darkness and light, heat and cold. His thoughts never stayed still and tears marked his shirt in shifts from the crying bouts. It wasn't until some days later, a dehydrated half dead man would be pulled from his catatonic state by the pounding on the door and the yelling of voices.

"Open up! This is the police. Is everything O.K.?

This sniper didn't move but slowly opened his eyes and saw his princess with blurred vision still lying on his lap. A soft whisper of a voice was all he could muster – "go away." The voices continued in the hall as they decided whether or not to break down the door. One man saying stand clear, and then pounding on the door. It shook and splintered into the foyer after a few shots. The men were inside with guns drawn going from room to room. They saw the two sitting there and were just as confused as he was some nights ago. How did this happen?

He would later be told that it had been 5 days before he was found. The hot and cold he felt was his body's limited recollection from the days and nights that had gone by while he was in an almost trance-like shock. The poor girl's body was beginning to rot through the heat of the summer days, and the open window made for ventilation to the rest of the complex. It wasn't long before neighbors noticed and complained to the landlord, who then came and tried to knock on the door with no luck. The cops were called in, and now there they were. Standing in the kitchen, calling for an ambulance and wondering what the hell happened.

The other tenants gathered round the front of the building to fulfill some morbid curiosity as the black body bag and the man on a stretcher were carried out, all murmuring to themselves and each other. He was too tired and out of it to care. His princess was gone.

CHAPTER FOUR

Bright yellow spinning discs, round and round on a black darkness – swirling slowly – her face in the center of each bright light, like miniature universes. Spinning faster and faster revolving swiftly now, the spin of the black bounding away, loosely dissolving into the distance. The lights were all gone now and only the darkness remained. The peaceful, quiet darkness.

Then coming out of it, coming to the surface – finding sight and hearing, listening to voices; slowly the eyelids open, regain focus, and the blurring recedes. A guard notices the eyes fluttering, then opening. He reaches over and pushes the intercom button and a voice answers.

"Yes, what can I do for you?"

"Can you get the doctor or nurse? The guy in here is waking up."

"Yes sir, right away."

The guard says "thanks" and the room returns to its silence. The man's eyes are closed again and the voices were hard to make out, still a million miles away. He tries to lean up and speak and gets a muffled, "Where am I?" whisper out.

"Hang in there, friend, the doc is coming."

The man sinks back into the bed, exhausted even from that exertion. He looks squarely at the guard when he speaks this time.

"My wife?"

The man knows the answer before the guard begins to speak. He knew before he even asked. Somehow he was hoping it was all some horrible nightmare, that he was in the hospital now from a car wreck, or even back in the war, and this had all been a bad dream. He knows from the moment the guard doesn't respond with confusion that it's all been true.

"I'm sorry about your wife. She died from internal bleeding. It didn't look like she ever made it to the phone. Docs were saying she didn't suffer long. They were talking about asthma or some lung problems ... maybe exaggerated from the city pollution ... said they would have to wait for you to wake up before they could find out any real answers ... "

The door knob lifted and in stepped the doctor, poised and ready for action. He had the usual white coat covering gray slacks and the white shirt, the half concealed stethoscope in the right hand pocket of the coat. Behind the black mustache and wire framed glasses, a serious mind is ready to respond to his patients' questions. Immediately he is recognized as "the doctor", but the question of who is this man lingers in the air.

"Hello, I am Steven and I am your doctor – how are you feeling?"

Achy, nauseous, all around like crap. If I break down I think I'm going to die, and that doesn't sound half bad right now.

"I'm alright. A little bit of a headache."

"Any dizziness? Nausea? Loss of ... "

"No, I feel fine. What about my wife?"

The doctor paused for a moment, some news always requires it, no matter how obvious it is or how many times it's been said. He took the ledger from the foot of the bed and began to browse it as he spoke, looking up occasionally.

"Well, as the officer told you, she died of internal hemorrhaging due to a coughing fit, most likely brought on by stress. All of this can be traced to her acute asthma which is a lung disorder ... "

"I know what it is."

"Right, of course you do. The combination of things ... the stress, the asthma, the amount of carbon monoxide in the air. The body can only take so much ... unfortunately, the state of the body ... so many days had passed before we were able to examine the body, therefore it is hard for us to make assumptions. I'm sorry."

The doctor was choosing his words carefully. The man he was speaking to was in rough shape physically, dehydrated and just out of a catatonic state that lasted several days and mentally, he obviously suffered a nervous breakdown upon finding his wide dead in the kitchen. And he hasn't changed that much over the 3 days, so it was a good time to think about the word choice.

"Everyone's sorry ... "

The man was speaking softly, with open hands on his bed, as he swayed his eyes from one side of the room to the other, tears welling and voice beginning to choke up.

" ... everyone's always sorry. They're sorry for me, they're sorry for the world, now they are sorry for her ... " He clenched his fists. He couldn't handle it all. He decided to fight the choke in his voice so he could keep talking and just let the tears drip down his face.

"I'm sorry ... "

"Who gives a shit that you are! My *wife* is dead! What are you going to do about that ... who is gonna take action ... "

The doctor looked somewhat startled but emotional outbursts, both of anger and joy, are not uncommon in a hospital. Now he regained what little composure he lost and tried to keep the man talking rationally.

"What do you mean, take action? What action do you think could be taken?"

"The damn pollution of the city caused her death, you just said that. Man and all his glorious technology ... "

"That's not quite what I meant ... "

"No of course not, not you. You can only hint around the truth. You can't actually get right down to it. You are part of it. If it weren't for cities of pollution where would your little hospital be? It would take quite a few sheep farms to equal how many people you see here. It's all about wealth and power. Everyone's sorry ... I'm sorry ... , I'm sorry. No you're not. You're part of it. You're part of the problem."

"I assure you, I am sorry for your loss. And you shouldn't forget that many lives are saved by the new advances that are made. This hospital is where I do see many patients, but I help a good number of them."

"Fine, doc, fine. The greatest good, right. Sacrifice the few so that the many will be saved. I get it. I know those odds. I wasn't the guy saving lives in some clean pretty hospital ... I was over there ... I was one of the people that was sacrificed for the many. But I went so that people like my princess didn't have to sacrificed. That was the whole goddamn point."

The doctor had nowhere to go. He wasn't involved in this man's life before today, and he wouldn't ever see him again after tomorrow. The man was angry and venting. Most people that see war have a lot to vent about.

"Your actions in the war, however noble and patriotic, cannot cure the ills of the world. You did your duty, and America thanks you for it. But you can't believe that the rest of life will be perfect from here on out."

The man waved off all the doc's "compassion" – he has seen more believable bedside manners in the jungle. Now he tried to redirect the doctor's attention to who would be held responsible for this lawlessness.

"My wife died because of pollution. Who do I talk to about taking action?"

"Again, I'm sorry about your wife, but I don't think you understand."

He moved closer to the bed as he talked and went into his teaching mode.

"Many times a person's life is shorter than it could have been due to unnecessary causes, such as stress or illness, or even, as in this case, a mixture of external forces, like pollution and illness and asthma. But this does not mean anyone can be sued, or recompense needs to be paid to ... "

"I don't want any money."

The interjection was one of indignation. To be noble by yourself is one thing, to be noble and misinterpreted for greedy and heartless was another.

"I don't want to sue anybody, you dumb ... "

He stopped himself, heated in the moment. He still needed this man's testimony if anything was going to be done. He began again, slower and steady. The storm just behind the calm.

"I want to make sure, that whoever *is* responsible for changing the amount of smog in this crappy place does suffer. It doesn't make much sense to me, that a person comes in and cause of death is known, and nothing is done to change it. Maybe I'm not understanding something."

"I'm afraid you are."

The doctor was done talking. This man had now gone far enough to be insulting as well as ignorant of how progress works. He scribbled some notes on the pad and put it back at the foot of the bed, admonished him to get rest, and was gone. The guard who had been silent there the whole time now rustled only an inch or two, but drew attention to himself. The man looked him up and down, realized he was his senior in mind by far more than years, and spoke to him kindly.

"So, are you gonna be here the whole time, like a personal guard?"

The officer half smiled and walked a step closer, glanced out the partially opened door, and then turned back to the bed.

"No. I'm just here to get a statement from you. Then I'll go."

Should have seen that coming.

"Not much to say, we had a fight, I walked out, went out to cool off. Stopped by a bar to have a drink or two, by the time I got back ... you know the rest."

"We thought it must have gone something like that, but had to get the statement from you. We also have to ask you not to leave town for a while, for the inquest, which will be scheduled as soon as I turn in my report."

The officer looked up from his pad and waited to see the man's eyes. His voice and demeanor had completely changed, from professional to comrade.

"I'm sorry about your wife.

"Thanks officer – I'm sure you mean it. Meanwhile, the doc over there ... I guess I'll just try to figure out what to do without any help here ... "

The officer half nodded, showing his agreement. Couldn't hurt to try. He happened to agree with both men, the widower and the doc. Seems two sides of the same coin, but it wouldn't hurt to try and rile things up a little on the down side. He walked through the door and shut it.

The man was left all alone again in the barren hospital room. Nothing there but his thoughts. The whole of what had happened sank its teeth into him again. His mind screamed and he wanted to escape, to find his love, to leave everything, to go away. Sleep took him and for a few moments he was at rest from exhaustion. But then, she was there. Accusing him, pointing the finger at him ... saying it was his fault.

"You did this to me. You helped them kill me. You were put here, in this darkness. I need you, but first you must set it right, you must set it right."

"No, I didn't ... I'm sorry, Princess. You're everything to me in this world."

"I was, but they killed me, little by little, they killed me. And now, they will try to kill you. They'll finish you the way they finished me. You must punish them for what they did to me. Do it for me. Do it for all who get trampled on. Bring the change ... you are the knight in shining armor, go and slay the dragons."

"Well, how are we this morning?"

The bright chipper nurse, asleep in her shining white outfit and shoes.

"Fine, nurse. When will I be able to go?"

"The doctor says you're over your shock and will be able to leave in about two days. Until then, just rest and take it easy."

"Rest and take it easy, that's what I've been doing, there's nothing else to do. Gives me time to think about what I'm going to do when I get out of here."

He was already chasing his own thoughts as he turned towards the window, far enough from the room that he didn't hear the nurse say that she thought it would be good to plan ahead.

CHAPTER FIVE

The alarm went off with a soft ting, ting, ting as "the man" as he was called by those that worked for him, reached over to shut it off. He was not big in stature, standing at 5'9" with a medium build and receding hairline. He was actually rather average. He was thinking about getting a hair transplant. It was an extravagance, but what the hell, it was his money and he was the one who broke his back to get it. Now he could do anything he wanted with it. At the moment it was getting ready to play a beautiful round of golf on a Saturday morning.

His wife called to him from the bedroom.

"Oh, do you have to go so early to play that ridiculous game? Why don't you stay here with me, nice and warm, under the covers?"

"Now, now. Golf is not a ridiculous game. It is a wonderful de-stressor for the tensions of a hard week and the perfect cap to a good one. You just go back to bed, and I'll be back by twelve or so. God knows, we've gone through enough hard times to warrant taking a few days off now and then."

She laughed softly. "I know, dear. Do you remember when we were so broke, you used to go out to the trash can every morning after the paper boy left and take one of the extra papers he had thrown away; then it was read, read, read the want ads. God what a time that was."

"Oh yes, I remember." He was still talking from in front of the bathroom mirror. "It seems like a million years ago sometimes, and then others ... like yesterday. Yes. I definitely remember. It was the experience that taught me something, taught me I don't like being broke."

He looked at her through the mirror as she rolled over onto her back to smile at him.

"You know, I look back on those days with a certain fondness. I really do. Maybe because I feel like it made me who I am today. Everything I am and have, I owe somehow to those hard times. Who knows? I sure wouldn't like to do it that way again."

"Even then, when we were broke most of the time, you used to give to different charities if you had a nickel in your pocket when we passed on the street." She had made her way from off the bed and was standing behind him now as she put her arm around his neck and shoulder and hugged him. "You always said that, unfortunately, there were people in the world worse off than you."

"I just figured we were healthy and smart. In a few years we would make it and have more than enough money. Some people ... well, some people don't have either."

"See. You are a sentimental goat underneath that big man exterior. You play tough, but you're just as soft as a pillow." She was teasing him now and being playful, perhaps in some small hope that the man she loved would stay home with her and throw his plans to the wind. "Sometimes I think you care more than you want to admit."

He smiled at her. He loved her and his life. Right now he was going to play golf, though.

"I will see you at twelve." He kissed her lightly on the forehead and made his way downstairs. He made some coffee and light breakfast and was on his way to the green.

The drive was short and enjoyable. He met his friends there with a smile and exclamation of what a beautiful day it was.

"Boys, today is special." He took a deep breath. "I can feel it. The sun is shining, the birds are singing. I'm feeling good. I think we are going to do things on this course that we've not done before."

The other men rolled with his positive mood and had fun answers all around.

"Yeah, like get a hernia carrying our bags?"

"Or rip our pants bending over ... "

The matching seemed to take only seconds.

"See? What'd I tell you? Coming off on top right in the beginning. Alright, no wise ass remarks. Just stand back, watch and learn. First, one places the tee thusly, placing the ball on top of it in a nice, gentle motion."

From that point, right when the ball was placed on the tee, everything began to wind down. The golfer's feet were 14 inches apart, just about underneath the shoulders, the arms came back to the top of the arch, holding a hanger, the breath was held, club raised and ready to strike. The "thwack" sound of hitting the ball was replaced with a similar "thuppck", but the ball never moved.

Pink and red exploded – caught by the sun and reflecting it as a painting of ocean waves. Bits of brain, skin and hair went flying through the air, landing on the ground all around the party. The bullet entered his head in the front of his left temple, and left with half of his head out on the opposite side. It was brutal, ugly, and over in a fraction of a second. "The man" was dead before he hit the ground, and no golf records were going to be made today. Not anymore. It could be said that he never heard the shot that killed him, but as the rest of the city was waking up, the frightening news was being played everywhere.

"Ladies and gentlemen, we interrupt our normal programming to bring you this very important news bulletin. At approximately 7:05

this morning, the President of Future Electronics was shot and killed. He was with friends at a private country club in the area, where he was a member. He was just beginning his customary nine holes this morning, when an assassin's bullet brought him down. One of our reporters is now on the scene with one of the members of the party who witnessed the murder. Back to you Johnny."

"Thank you. Here on the course there is confusion and chaos, but at the same time a strange, morbid quiet. The police have the situation in hand, and the ambulance removed the body some 40 minutes ago. I have with me one of the persons who witnessed the sudden death. Tell me, what was it like, what happened?"

A small man in a plaid jacket, yellow pants and white golf shoes spoke into the microphone hesitantly.

"It was bad ... it was over so fast. He never knew what hit him ... he was saying this morning before we teed off, today he was going to do things he had never done before ... Jesus ... "

The news commentator took the mike back, halting the man's public reflections.

"Tragic. That's the story from the course. Back to the studios."

"Thanks, Johnny. The police have no clues yet as to the killer's identity. It is thought, however, that this killing is connected to the other killings that have been plaguing the city for the past year. Although there is no substantial proof, all the killings were done from a distance. This unfortunately ruins the bullets' ballistic value as the further the distance a bullet flies, the more damage it sustains when it reaches the target. In cases such as these, the bullets are of little help, being almost completely destroyed. The police are having a very difficult time determining exactly what type of weapon is being used, and therefore cannot say conclusively whether the murders are in fact, linked."

"The police have hypothesized that the weapon used was most likely a rifle with an oversized cartridge, and the killer fired from a quarter mile away from his victims. This murderer, whoever he is, is certainly a good marksman."

The news man continued, dragging out every last bit he could, more people were listening to him than ever before.

"Another curious link, the twelve men murdered all held high positions in their respective companies. That ends our special news bulletin. If we receive any further word, we will interrupt our scheduled programming to bring it to you first. Now back to our 'music – to relax to.'"

CHAPTER SIX

The hand that turned off the radio was calm and steady. Alone in the bare apartment, he began talking aloud.

"Well, that's that, my fat little friends. Thing are getting just a little tight for me. It's getting tougher and tougher to keep your greedy 'heads of dynasties' rolling. I was lucky today; almost didn't get away. I barely got my rifle apart before people were at the scene. To think what would have happened if I hadn't brought my golf bag stuff to play the role. I just moseyed off the course, but it could have been in cuffs."

It was a shadow of the man he was only a few short years ago. Time, it seems, did not believe in equality. Skinnier and more pale, but with an irreversible distance in his eyes and thoughts. Even if he looked right at you, you were not there.

He no longer killed for King and Country. Now he killed for Justice, and that does something to a man. Every time you pull the trigger, it is for a reason, and if that reason remains outside of yourself, like your government, or your country, or your superior officer, or an attacker – any of those, you never got tangled up in it yourself. In fact, if you remove all those reasons, if you are able to, then you won't feel the desire to kill and may have a hard time dealing with what those things made you do. But now, now it was him. It was all him. He decided who to kill, and when. He decided who deserved to die, based on his justice. The world had set these men free and paid them handsomely; now he was delivering his verdict, personally. His mind currently raced through the earlier scene, reliving the events of the morning.

The man walked quickly back to his car, just a few meters away. Swiftly, yet with care, he took the rifle down, putting it disassembled into the golf bag. As he stood with the golf bag beside him, his trunk key half-turned in its lock, glancing over his appearance, he heard a car driving up. The first thing he saw were the blue lights on the top of the car, as it pulled to a stop immediately beside his.

His hands started to swear with the possible alternatives running through his mind. He could run, drop the act and say the car was stolen; he could kill the officer, chances are this little bastard never saw death like he has and wouldn't stand a chance; he could wait, give the officer his license and just play it smooth. By the time the last possibility had run its course, he could see the officer reach over to his microphone and call it in. Badge number, location, status – checking the plate to see if it was hot.

Slowly, he reached deeper into his pocket and felt the cool handle of the .45 pocket Derringer in his moist hand. He found it in a small pawn shop a few years ago and never regretted the price, carrying it with him all these years everywhere he went since the service – now he was very pleased with the purchase.

"Good morning, Officer."

The officer was walking towards him, sizing him up like it would be a fist fight, and thinking he would win. Kids these days just don't have respect for their elders.

"Morning, sir. You're going to have to move your car; it's parked too close to that fire hydrant there." He pointed over to the fire hydrant, blatant, with no cover bushes anywhere near it.

"Gee. You sure are right, aren't you? Guess I just didn't notice, I'm sorry. You know if *my* house was on fire, I wouldn't want some guy parked in front of this thing either."

"Yeah, well, that's the way people are – if it doesn't affect them, if it's not their place burning down, they just don't think about it."

The office was making small talk but it wasn't friendly chit chat, more of a lesson. But this banter was removing suspicion, and this topic was one that he could write a book on, the officer just opened the door.

"You know, you are absolutely right. It's the simple little considerations in life. Just yesterday, I was driving home, and it was 4:40, and there's traffic, like always, and an ambulance is trying to get through. Nobody wants to move; like they are going to lose their space in the traffic, right. They were just going home, and they weren't in an ambulance going to the hospital; that was the stranger right next to them! And they still didn't want to do it. I tell ya ... "

The officer was looking for a way out of this can of worms, when his radio inside the cruiser sounded loudly. He turned over his shoulder quickly glancing at it, as if it was the criminal himself coming through the speakers. The words were jumbled amidst the usual static, but the man had a pretty good idea about what the officer just missed. He looked over to play up the importance of the information and the office was turning it back into his classroom and dismissing everyone.

"Gotta go – play it cool and move the car."

He stood patiently as he watched the officer get into his cruiser, pick up the radio, speak a few short words into the microphone, listen intently to the reply, start the engine, flip on the lights and screech away.

Sirens sounded outside the window now, a little farther off, but the same sirens. *Policia.* Who knows, maybe even the same officer. He looked out the opened window at the brick building across the way, over the murmuring people below, and began talking aloud again.

"Yeah, that was a close one. Almost had to make a decision that would not have been easy. Now I'm all jumpy, like too much adrenaline pumping through me. Sure, I talk well, talked him right back into his cruiser and he never suspected a thing. But what if he had gotten that news before I set the tone? I would have been suspect number 1, and I would have had a hell of a time talking my way out of that without anything short of killing him. We are both lucky, then. It was a bit close."

The slender figure moved away from the bed and window and sunk into a chair in the living room. Although emotionally and physically weary from the strain of the morning's events, his mind was too active about any one thing. For a moment his monologue stopped being nervous and began to fill with happy pride in his accomplishments and the disarray he had created.

"I had better lay off the big guys for a while. It's going to be wild around here. I bet those bastards are going to be scared to step outside. Maybe I can work out a plan to take out some small fries – the little jerks who help the big ones get away with everything, hoping one day to be the big man themselves ... Aw, what the hell. I can't think of this right now. I'll watch some boob tube for a while – see what stimulating edifying program is on. First though, I'll get some soda and take a piss."

Leaving the T.V. on, he headed toward the bathroom, nonchalantly walking by open windows without a care in the world. No one had seen him, no one even knew anything about "the sniper". Literally, if he played his cards right, and never played sloppy, he could do this forever.

"That feels good."

He washed his hands and went into the kitchen to fulfill the second part of the task for the evening, opened the refrigerator, paused for a moment in front of it, pondering if he would like a sandwich to go with it.

"I think I will have a sandwich with it."

He began singing to himself as he took out the bread, cold cuts and fixings. He brought out the pickles and soda as his appetite was reawakened by the sight of food. After making his plate, he reclaimed his seat in front of the television and turned it on to the news.

" ... but Congress has declined to pass the bill regarding the amount of exhaust and toxicity allowed, because as a few Representatives have stated, the bill is too watered down; they really have no bill to pass."

And, on the local scene – well. Moms and dads – in about two weeks, you can expect your little ones to be out of school for the day and begging you to take them to see the astronauts. Yes, that's right. These are the same astronauts who go up and around the globe and they will be right here in town as part of an exhibition to educate and entertain. The Mayor has asked that all places of business, both public and private, close for the day to honor this great country and some of its finest. He has requested that if any businesses do remain open, any and all personnel are permitted to see the astronauts without penalty, if they choose. There will be a parade, as well as speeches by the Mayor and other honoraries in honor of the astronauts. The local bands that will participate ... "

The figure eating his sandwich had stopped eating, mid-bite. Food in mouth, he now listened attentively to every word the newsman said. A smile moved slowly across his face, finally bursting in a triumphant laugh.

"Oh MAN, that's it! That's great. Oh boy, oh boy ... that's just the deal I've been looking for. All those little creeps out there with their kids, yelling and screaming, and the people all out of work, all in one big mass, trying to get to see 'the big parade.' The streets will be flooded, parents chasing their little darlings this way and that. The cops will have their hands full with everything from crowd control to pick pockets."

Already he was up and began to clear the kitchen table, moving his half eaten sandwich and the remaining soda back into the refrigerator. The rest of the clutter found its way to an unused seat. He needed to find a map of the city and find out the parade route – where the speeches would be given. They would be like sitting ducks for an untrained Joe Schmoe hunter; for him this was like Christmas, and every present under the tree had some highbrow glutton's name on it.

"Maybe I can get those little fuckers after all."

CHAPTER SEVEN

"Pardon me, ma'am. Could you please tell me where I can get the information on which route the parade is going to take? I have a 7 year old, and he is so excited about these astronauts coming."

"Yes, I believe there is a map around here somewhere that will show you exactly which streets will be used ... " She began shuffling through her papers as he stood idly by. Put a smile on and you brighten up a person's day. " ... Wouldn't you know, just when you are looking for something, that's when you can't find it."

For a moment he thought it ironic that she was going to feel bad if she couldn't help him with the location of the parade route. Then he noticed she was feeling embarrassed at her lack of organization. She looked very efficient in her navy dress with white cuffs, but her smile reviled her nervousness. She obviously enjoyed her work at the information center, talking to the pleasant people seeking help and answers. Now, as she moved stacks of booklets and pamphlets looking for the maps she hurried – probably because this gentleman was so pleasant.

"Oh yes, here it is. Now as you can see ... right here ... the parade is going to cut through the center of town, turn down Elm Street, cross through the park and then stop here for the speeches."

She was just as animated in her description of the route as she was in trying to find it, especially since the work was done and the customer had been satisfied. Now his light answers and questions would be very well received, and slide without any attention.

"Yes, yes, I see. Thank you very much, miss. My kids have been after me to take them to it, but I had no idea where it was going to be routed. May I keep this?"

"Oh my, yes. We have plenty. We knew people would be coming in here for those so we had quite a few printed up."

He nodded in appreciation and expressed his gratitude once again before leaving, no sooner had the door closed behind him than the young woman began telling a co-worker what a polite man he was. Once outside, he hurried along the street. Even though the sun was shining brightly and the weather was beautiful, he was anxious to get home. Inside the familiar surroundings he felt more at ease. He flung his jacket onto a living room chair and spread the map out on the kitchen table.

"So, here's the map with all the answers ... "

He used some glasses as paperweights for the corners and then grabbed one more for himself. He opened the fridge and took a bottle of orange soda from the door and poured a glass, then started drinking it in large gulps, "ahhhh"-ed and then went back to the map and talking out loud.

"Alright ... so let's see ... the parade is going to start here ... then go down the main drag ... O.K ... .then cross to the right behind this row of buildings ... and then stopping right at the speaker's platform."

His hand was tracing the path on the 2-D map on the table, but his mind was in the real world cruising down the road watching the parade from all angles like a free roaming camera, pausing and rewinding when desired.

"Hmm ... this building is the old One Grove Street building ... probably the biggest one at the corner ... it's been mostly vacant for some time ... some units rented though ..."

He traced the route over and over on the map and in his mind, thinking, working in a rhythm as his finger moved over the piece of paper. The room was silent except from the sound of his breathing and the slight rustle of the paper. Minutes passed before his finger came to a stop in one corner of the map. One building in particular seemed fit for his purpose, and although the map was somewhat inscrutable regarding the actual types of buildings and their size, it appeared that he may have found what he was looking for. The structure looked to be a single building facing the entrance to the park, directly overlooking the parade route.

What exactly he was planning was unraveling in his own mind, whether or not to open rapid fire or simply snipe the ones as they ran, perhaps some massive explosion; the possibilities all seemed quite good. He stared for several minutes, with a smile that came and faded and came back and then disappeared again as the endless array of possible destructions came to him.

Leaving his map folded on the kitchen table, he walked slowly to the chair where he flung his coat nearly an hour ago, put it on and started toward the door. He stopped momentarily with his hand on the handle, thinking the last thoughts of the map before he went out to examine the 2D version and then left, leaping down the stairs in bounds. The sun was still shining brightly when he opened the front door of the downstairs foyer and stepped outside. The map firmly memorized, he had no trouble finding his way to the spot where the designated building stood. As he looked around it, he found himself alone on the street, although it was an off shoot of the main drag. Now the optimistic thoughts began to fly through his head.

"Fantastic ... there it is. An old hotel or something; the 'Andorra.' Whatever the hell that means. Standing solid and tall with nothing around it. Looks like they knocked down all the surrounding buildings not too long ago ... this one probably has a due date as well. The last one to go. Lucky for me."

He was making his way toward the face of the building, searching systematically with his eyes for the condemned building's entrance. Amongst all the rubble, it wasn't an easy find, and no easier to get to as he stumbled through all the debris and loose rocks. At that moment, a figure in uniform came from around the corner and spoke, startling him. He was so into his thoughts, that he had not heard the man walking up.

"Hey there young fella, hold on."

Having no idea who the man was or what he was doing there, the man answered cautiously. Ignorance and casual friendliness are always your allies when playing down suspicion.

"Huh? What is it? Something the matter?"

"You can't go around there, it's too dangerous. Everything's been torn down. Didn't you see the sign up at the start of the street? No one's to come down this way ... that's why it's so quiet around here."

"I did see some knocked over sign, but I couldn't really read it. I sure wouldn't have come down here if I'd known that. I don't want to break the law or anything."

The old man was truly looking out for him. A strange kindness from a stranger, indeed. Playing it down was simple enough and the old man was trusting, admiring him almost, if only for his youth.

"You don't need to worry about that. I'm the only one that's here when the wrecking crew isn't on site, like a watchman, and I'm the only one. The crew won't start back up until after the parade's gone through, like a mini-vacation, and until then it's my job to make sure no one comes round here and gets hurt, mostly kids and all. But I don't want you getting hurt and getting me fired either, so just be careful."

The sniper was still walking and surveying the building and surroundings as he spoke. The old man was harmless enough. Besides with their repertoire now, he may even have some information that would be useful.

The watchman was looking from the younger man to the building and back. In the end, the two men sharing company wasn't really that far off for either one of them. Both in their own worlds, and the other just close enough on the horizon so you don't have to battle the idea of complete isolation from society.

"It feels sad sometimes, but it's growth and progress. Can't fight it. The new ways replace the old, and the people without any ties to these old buildings knock 'em down and build some new ones, that will inevitably face the same fate."

He was solid looking now, calm and collected. He seemed to get younger the more he talked. Apparently, the young man's guise of ignorance was not the only costumed aired for protection from the unknown. He wasn't that old, just lived long and played it up. The younger man had actually stopped evaluating the grounds for the moment and was purely looking at the man and listening to his story. He was more an equal than he had bumped into in some time. The progress doesn't leave anyone unscathed, was the final thought he rested on before he spoke coolly to the old man.

"Say ... sir. Would you be alright if I went to the top – to look around?"

There is a way people can ask questions that are not really questions, more polite informational statements. There is a certain amount of respect in doing so and the world becomes a wordless place of mutual respect. The world is very limited as the people that can perceive this world are growing small, and those that follow its rule of conduct with conviction even fewer.

"Well, I don't know. It's pretty dangerous ... .lots of hidden holes and bad falls for a misstep."

And so the subliminal conversation continued as the old man's admonishments were not saying "no," as much as they were saying "be extra careful."

The younger man nodded in acknowledgment of this understanding and said he "would be extra careful" before he headed toward the abandoned building.

CHAPTER EIGHT

The watchman stood there for a moment as he pushed open the front door. As he disappeared inside, the older man walked away nervously, yet tried to appear confident in his trust.

Inside the hotel, he pushed aside some boards that lay in his path. In the dim light he moved out of the entrance-way into the main lobby. The bar for signing in still had the bell to ring for assistance. Since out of earshot he rang it softly, rang it twice on his way by and began talking to himself.

"Now let's see, if I were stairs, where would I be?"

The elevator obviously wouldn't be working anymore, but the stairs wouldn't be that far. He moved toward the rear of the lobby, where the three elevator shafts stood. The place was covered with dust and disheveled. Cobwebs hung from the ceiling and chairs alike. Life has stopped here and nothing was left by the memories, and the stories that would never be told. The elevator doors were open; dust had covered the floor surfaces everywhere that was exposed. Rust had taken its toll on any metal that was there, and demolition was probably cheaper than rehabilitation.

He moved past the elevators to a door marked "EXIT." He pushed the jammed door, then gave it a kick to get it open. It slammed open, its sound echoing in the empty room. The stairs and walls in the stairwell were chipped and worn. As he walked up each flight, he considered the old man's views and the last words the old man said before he disappeared into the windowless foyer, "just be careful – from one guy who remembers to another, be careful."

"Now, hopefully, these will lead right to the roof." He leaned over the rail and looked up all the flights. "This is going to be fun carrying all my gear. Not like I haven't sweat before. Well, hotel, looks like you are going to have a new resident – what's that you say – no charge? Well, that is most generous."

He climbed flight after flight until he reached what appeared to be the last flight and then looked for another opening. A heavy metal door, just a few steps into a corridor, leading up one more flight and out to the roof.

"What a climb! Phew. Thank God."

He rested by the door with one hand on the handle and the other hand on his leg, supporting his upper body weight as he took deep breaths. He pushed the heavy door and it seemed welded shut. Leaning heavily against it, he pushed it open, slowly breaking the years of rust inch by inch. The door squeaked and moaned as he repeatedly shouldered it open before he called it quits, giving himself about 13 inches clearance. He stood up straight and walked out directly over to the edge.

"Beautiful, just beautiful, what a sight."

The wind came up and blew gently around him, and the evening sun cast its warmth on his face. He could see all the nearby town below and the cars passing and the people walking up further streets. For the moment he was a man admiring the view as he circled the roof, looking out with appreciation and fondness for the world. All of that melted away when he reached the spot where he would be able to see the parade, and events began to unfold in his mind.

"At least three-quarter of a mile view from up here, mild wind. The stand is going to be there, and the parade is going to come up from over there and stop there. Man, with a decent scope, I could pick people off up to a mile away. In fact, with this view, even when hell breaks loose, I could probably get them in a crowd, if in all their nobility that's where they take cover."

He turned and began making his way back toward the stairway door. His feelings were dead to the wind blowing softly around him, and the sun was no longer warming his body. His thoughts were of days to come, and he still remained positive about the roof of the building, but his voice was empty now as he opened the door.

"This is beautiful, just beautiful. Couldn't have asked for a better set up."

He moved back through the heavy half-open door and cautiously groped his way down the several flights of stairs, carefully avoiding the rubble. As he emerged into the sunlight, the watchman was walking slowly toward the door of the hotel. He looked up at him and the sniper smiled a sincere smile.

"Hey, thanks, mister. I really appreciate that view. I can't thank you enough."

He waved it off and smiled back.

"Oh, it's nothing. Glad to be of some help. Well, take care now."

He watched the young man go, walking quickly with a lightness in his step, almost like a visible happiness. "I don't know who he is," the old man thought, "but he's a nice man; short hair, not like those kids these days and clean clothes, no dirty jeans. Polite. Said he remembered the area, funny, I don't recall a lemon-ice stand around here.

He tried to think on it a moment, then shrugged his shoulders as he dismissed it and turned back to his job, as the man disappeared in the distance down a street.

The store was small, but looked like a thriving business. It was similar to the stores in the city – small, unpretentious outside, and inside the business boomed. There was a sign above the door that read in big red hand-written letters:

GOOD RIFLES BOUGHT AND SOLD

AMMO AND HUNTING EQUIPMENT

IF YOU DON'T SEE IT – ASK!!

Inside, a nondescript customer was halfway through a small and not unusual purchase.

"Yessir, that's right – two of these boxes of 30 caliber ammunition and couple of those batteries right over there, as well. Yep, those. And what's that all come to?"

The clerk totaled the purchase on the register, took the bill offered and returned the man's change, and began describing his self-evident actions out of habit.

"Thank you, sir. Let me put this in a bag for you and you will be all set."

He packed the few items up without order, and turned away disinterestedly as the customer walked out of the store, ringing the little bells above the door as he exited. Once outside the man turned quickly to the right still looking at a downward angle and headed up the street. It was a clear day, but the air was heavy. The man sighed and began to mumble to himself as he walked along. He seemed unrecognizable, as was his intent. He had worn different casual outfits to several different stores, that was the third one today.

"At least no one is going to pay attention to someone buying a couple boxes of ammo. And if they do try to track it down, they will have their hands full. Every store will have a record of similar purchases. I am getting tired from all this walking, though. Think I'll head home after one more store and get out the rifle equipment – still need to pack it all up."

Carrying all his packages under his arm, he took the stairs two at a time, the adrenaline of excited anxiety driving him. He unlocked the door and closed it and locked it again quietly behind him, leaning against it, he stood there – almost in relief. He had spent more and more time in his apartment by himself, and going out even for the necessities seemed to be unbearable.

"It's good to be home."

He took the packages into the kitchen, placing them carefully on the table. His jacket landed on the familiar chair in the living room, and he immediately went to the closet to pull out his rifle. There, in the bottom of a clothes bag, neatly packed in an ebony box, lay his sword of justice. He gently removed the rifle and the scope from the case. As always, he handled it with fondness and respect; admiring the power of the two combined – the man and the rifle make a formidable weapon. With the added sniper scope, they are practically unbeatable.

Like a strong marriage, the man is the custodian of the rifle, and the rifle the safe keeper of the man. The unity takes time, months and months of training and understanding. Years later, you still have room to learn more and become closer – better together. Some men can't seem to understand how the rifle will react to the different situations; sight is dependent on wind or rain; how the breech behaves in high humidity, how much pressure to apply to the trigger before she goes. Then the self-reflection, the complete knowledge of one's self in high tension situations – things you can't learn without the experience of them; things that if you fail to learn, will cost you your life.

And not every marriage is good or ends happily. The union had been totally satisfying, the man cared greatly for the weapon and treated it so, and the rifle had served the man well, bringing him home alive.

CHAPTER NINE

It's the day – the day – it had finally arrived. That night he would position himself on the roof and the next morning the accounts would be closed. He rested on the couch, hoping to get some sleep, only so the day would pass more quickly and the night would begin. The clock on the wall moves in spurts and jumps, seeming to stand still when his eyes are open but then jump as much as 45 minutes sometimes when he closes them. In his half dream-like state, lying on the couch, princess comes to him, telling him to be careful, that what he is doing may not have to be done this way, but he must be careful if he does it.

When he awakens, he feels good, excited and sure he is doing the right thing, the only just thing. Gone forever was the man that was able to take perspective on the acts and thoughts, replaced with the avenger that only sought justice, his justice. The knight in shining armor had disappeared as well, for he was part of the man, an idea that needed society to survive. A knight is part of it all, the people, the politics, the problems; believing in chivalry and justice as ideas but not perpetuating them, just riding it out. Now, the singular vigilante remained, created out of his own will and propelled by his own thoughts and actions.

The remainder of the day passes slowly, but when the night comes, it falls fast. The air darkens and the air grows chilly, as if the gods themselves are angry for what is going to happen. To the sniper as he begins his journey, it is just a crisp night.

"You know God, you and me have a lot in common. You gave up your son so that sins of man would be forgiven – I gave up my wife, not willingly of course, but she's gone just the same, and nothing got changed. You'd think that you'd of seen that one coming."

He was talking as he looked up occasionally at the sky. The dark matter silently starting back at him as he spoke. He was always religious, and now in his isolation, he believed more than ever in the idea of God, and the stories they tell about what this God has done and means to people; how he created the universe and will always be.

"Seems to me, the flood idea was pretty good. You just tell one person, one family, who is good, who stands by your ways, that it's coming, and then just wash the rest away. I'm not much of a sinner or a saint, God. But let your will be done."

The man stopped walking and looked up now as if some sort of answer would be given or some flood would happen. There was a sick desperation in his conversation, and he wished it wasn't one way.

"Fine. Fuckin' fine. You want to do it this way. You want me to be the only one here setting things straight – no sweat off me, jack. I got enough bullets here to kill every motherfucker at that parade tomorrow. I don't give a shit – everyone gets washed away in the big flood, right? Like Noah or whatever the hell the guy's name was, didn't like some of the people that died right before his eyes – his neighbors, his family, his friends, coworkers – I don't even know these assholes ... "

He had dropped his gear in the alleyway halfway through the tirade and was flailing about, swinging his arms with emotion. Standing now with clenched fists and eyes closed, with tears welling – all of this, and he saw the flash of light through his eyelids. The lightning filled the sky and thunder rumbled through the air. The man unclenches his fists, breathes deeply and opens his eyes. Again he feels the breeze cool his anger, and knows what he must do.

It's three in the morning and a derelict is stumbling drunkenly less than 200 yards from the base of the hotel. He's all over the sidewalk, and off of it ... walking with a looseness common to overindulgence. He has unknowingly caught the attention of the watchman, who currently is thinking the situation out.

"Boy, that guy sure has put one on. If he doesn't watch it, he's going to break his fool neck ... " As if on cue with his thoughts, the drunk hits a crack in the sidewalk, stumbles and goes face forward to the ground, arms uselessly flying. The watchman is now done debating with himself over what to do, and kindness takes control. He hurries over to the prostrate figure, puts an arm under his shoulder and heaves the drunk up.

Just as he gets him to his feet and smiles at the half conscious figure, his eyes light up as a growl escapes from the drunk's lips. The drunk, in a single movement, places his left arm around the watchman's neck, to stop an outcry as the right hand raises and plunges the knife it was concealing into his chest, and again into the heart of the mouth of the pained and surprised dying old man. He reaches up with the other hand and forces the old man to the ground on his back, as he takes his last few breaths, eyes frantically searching before they relax and roll back.

The sniper deposits the body in a hole behind the watchman's shack, one which he had seen from the roof earlier that day. He then collects his gear from the alleyway where he had placed it a few minutes before, and begins the climb to the roof. The ascent, with all the gear, takes a little over four minutes. Once out on the roof, he chooses for the occasion early morning hours. He will attempt to sleep, for he knows in a few short hours, he will need his strength and skill.

Less than forty minutes later, the rain begins to fall. He rests beneath the poncho, trying to keep warm and dry, trying to get sleep, as his mind wanders back and forth through time ... .

CHAPTER TEN

Dawn came, the sun bursting through the clouds, red everywhere, like the whole town was covered with blood. The sniper awoke, shook out his blanket and poncho, and started checking his equipment.

"Well, today is the day. Yessir, it will be a beautiful day. Now let's see, what did I decide the best plan of action was? Wait until the end of the parade when they are milling around like sheep? And I was going to hit one from each family group? Right, one from each group. That way no one goes home empty handed, and everyone will have something to remember from today. If I was to take out one family, how long would the whole of society mourn? How long would this town remember this day? BUT, if I take one person away from every group – everyone will remember. Jesus may have died for the sins of man two thousand years ago, but today, man dies from his own. No scapegoat this time."

He slowly circle the roof as he spoke, scanning the horizon from each side of the building. Focusing on the route of the parade again and watching it come in his mind's eye. He backed away from the edge of the roof, hitting his head on an antenna that was sticking to the side of the roof door exit.

Maybe the tension of the situation was finally getting to the sniper. He swore in anger and ripped it down from the wall with his bare hands and slammed it to the ground. He rubbed his head as he looked down at it. As his anger cooled he kneeled beside it, and recognized it as his own. He had the exact same model when he had lived with his princess, a long time ago, in a far far away land.

As he sat and mulled over his past, the rest of the town began to awake and get on with their day. The bright red dawn did not shine only for the old hotel roof, and it seemed the whole world around him was already preparing as well.

"Honey, the watch commander just called – he's sorry but the regular beat man hasn't showed, and you're next to cover a mandatory. He wants you to foot patrol near and around the condemned buildings, you know – near the parade route – he doesn't want any kids wandering through there and getting hurt."

"That's a crap story ... it's because I'm a rookie – I don't even think there is a list of shift coverage. Bullshit."

"What's that dear? Did you say something?"

He shook his head to himself and got his boots on. No reason to complain, he thought. Another couple of months and he wouldn't have to worry about it anymore – he'd be considered a regular old vet and all the junk detail would disappear. His wife, who he finds very attractive, comes in and he realizes that there is a worse fate that could have befallen him. He kisses her as he walks past and slaps her behind.

"Another busy day, then? Watching buildings! I can just hear my son telling the story of his policeman dad – well, he watches buildings. That's right, all day."

They both smile and the humor is light, it's a beautiful day and the parade would be fun to watch since the buildings weren't going to be hard to keep an eye on.

"Alright gang ... let's get up and at 'em. Wake up wake up. Your father's getting dressed. You know he canceled his trip so that we could be together today and go to the parade and then have a picnic afterward ... so let's go, c'mon."

"Aw mom, just a few more minutes," the young boy pleads, "we are growing boys and our bodies need the extra sleep." With that said he snuggles back under the covers, shielding his eyes from the sunlight let in by the now open blinds.

"Well, your bodies should have thought of that last night, and listened to your mom and gone to bed instead of staying up to watch that horror movie."

"It wasn't horror, it was science fiction ... "

"Well, either way, you've had your extra minutes. Now get up and go down to the kitchen and have some breakfast. We aren't going to eat again until late afternoon, after the parade is over."

By the time the children made it to the kitchen, it was the mom that had fallen behind pace, and they were not half as lenient it seemed.

"Hurry up with the chow mom, we need to get there early so we can get a good spot to see the ASTRONAUTS!"

She smiled at her child's enthusiasm and kidded with them.

"You are going to have to wait another minute – your eggs don't have the same affection for astronauts you do, and they aren't cooking faster. Anyway, who wants to go to space? What's there to look for a million miles away?"

The kids were like white on rice on this one.

"MOM! There are like a MILLION reasons to go to space. Man is the only animal with a brain, a brain that has a thirst for knowledge. If that thirst was stopped, the human race would cease to exist and we'd go back to being animals. IF there was no new frontiers to explore, what would we do? We'd go back to being animals, that's what."

For a moment, she contemplated what he had said for its insight and wondered where he had picked that up. She handed them their food and thought of how to answer her son, then she did answer him, chiding him but this time a little more serious as to what the government could be doing besides fulfilling the goal of exploration for the act of exploration itself.

"Well, there are a lot of problems right here on planet Earth, you know. People suffer from things like war and hunger, disease, pollution – lots of things could use the help right here, never mind all the millions of miles away."

The kids were eating their food and shaking their head like their mom just "didn't get it" again and she sighed and let it go. At least they were eating their eggs and it was a beautiful morning, birds chirping and all.

In another house, a wife was finishing the last breakfast preparations as her husband came stumbling out of the bedroom. Tired and beat.

"I don't know if I can make it to the parade today, this old body is just a little tired this morning."

She looked up from the plates and knew right away he was only complaining but was still keeping his promise of taking her. She smiled as she spoke to him as her excitement for the day was nearly uncontrollable.

"Bull ... you old phoney. You shouldn't have stayed out as late as you did with the 'boys' last night. You knew I was going to make you take me."

Still leaning against the door jamb with his eyes half closed, his reply was undaunted as he persisted in the game they were playing.

"Well, unfortunately, I guess I am not as young as I thought I was. I can't go out partying up 'til the late hours of eleven o'clock like last night anymore – it's just too much for me. Now I know, and will act accordingly for the future. Just a shame it's going to take its toll on today ... just a shame."

He was shaking his head and she was beginning to buy the story and feel a little worried. She knew he was only fooling, but there was one way to make sure he was up for it. She put the pan down and waltzed over to her man standing in the door way and played back.

"That's really too bad. I was so excited for the day that I have all this extra energy and I was hoping you would be able to help me use some of it up. But if you just aren't up for it, I guess I'll have to take a longer shower is all ... all by myself."

She walked passed him and rubbed his chest as she passed, smiling into his eyes that he pretended to have half closed, and went into the bedroom and began to prepare for a shower. He watched her for only a moment before smiling ear to ear and leaving the tired act behind and running up to her and picking her up in his arms.

"Well, maybe I'm still in the same shape I used to be after ... "

The last minute preparation at City Hall, the police departments and the like were running on smoother by comparison, but mostly because it had been prearranged weeks before. No parade to honor the astronauts and possibly get the town – and mayor – on national news was going to be left to chance and the wind. Every effort was made to make this a special and notable day, without glitches.

"Mr. Mayor, pardon the interruption, I just wanted to inform you that everything is on schedule. The bands are in place, the communications network is set and checked, and the media personnel have all been tagged and are on the scene."

The Mayor smiled at the intern as he thought about the possible coverage going state to state. It was a beautiful day, and it was only going to get better. He brushed him off with "that's great, son" and returned to the task of memorizing the last few lines of his speech. He had this opportunity to make a good impression and use this as a propelling factor for the next election, if all went well.

"Of course," he thought, "if it didn't go well, well, it was the first thing on the list to use against you – the Mayor that couldn't even host a parade without problems. That's never an easy problem to dodge. But life's about chances – can't win if you don't play. The last mayor found that out the hard way when he wouldn't accept the 'donations' to help campaign for votes in exchange for a more lenient environmental bill. No re-election there." He understood the way things worked, though. One little bill wouldn't have any lasting effects; wouldn't hurt anybody, least of all him.

The early morning hours in the emergency room were quiet, in stark contrast to the rush and urgency of the evening and late night hours. The day shift came on at seven thirty and was now enjoying a short coffee break before the eleven o'clock rush, passing the time with idle talk amongst close coworkers.

"Christ. I've been on for eighteen hours ... and I still have six more to go. I should have never taken that intern's shift."

"Now, now, doctor. We all know you are a decent, All-American boy with a heart of gold, and rather than see a poor, young man die of a broken heart because he couldn't meet with his fiancé's plane when it arrived, you did the only noble thing your heart would allow ... "

"Oh yes. True love ... or sex ... whichever governed my thoughts at the time. I'll tell you what. After this shift is over, I'll feel all good and honorable, but right now I could kill him for suckering me into this ... probably doesn't even have a fiancé. All I need is some disaster to strike, some small earthquake or ten-car-pile-up, then my day would be complete."

"Well, the paper here says it's going to be cloudy and might even rain again. See that. If you had the day off, you probably would have gone to the parade and been caught in the rain and ruined one of your suits."

"'Cause I always wear my nicest suits to parades ... "

"Exactly. So it's like it's your lucky day ... we should go to the casino when you get off."

They both smiled and half chucked at their own banter. The doctor working the double glanced out the window and the cloudy sky and shrugged. "Well," he thought, "at least if it rains people will stay inside and be less likely to hurt themselves." He turned around to find his colleague engrossed in the middle of the paper with his coffee in hand. As he walked by he patted him on the shoulder. "Wishful thinking, doc. Somebody is bound to come along and spoil that dream."

At the abandoned site, where the sniper lay dormant on the rooftop, the rookie is taking his second trip around his beat. He notices a truck with tanker in tow has pulled over to the side of the street, and walked over.

"Hey buddy. What's the matter? Engine trouble? You can't park here, is all. Gonna have to move."

"I know, I know. I was driving along fine then the gear slipped out. I can't move the mother son-of-a-gun out of here because I can't get it in gear. I already called the office and they're sending a mechanic down to fix her right away."

"Well, I hope your mechanic hurries it up and fixes it so you can get it moving. We have a parade coming through here in a couple of hours, and this could cause a real hassle if it's still here."

"Well, I'll let them know to put the pedal down, officer. They said they were sending him right down."

The officer stood back a little from the cab and perused the tanker as it sat still. Always was a truck man himself, and the driver seemed friendly enough. No need to hassle him too hard. He's done all he can, really. Now everyone just has to wait.

"You know, I've always been curious, how many gallons do you carry?"

The driver was still somewhat preoccupied with getting his truck started again before that parade paraded on through. He looked out from the cab and saw the officer just hanging out looking at his tanker and figured talking to him was better than the risk of a ticket right now. He jumped down from the cab and looked from the same angle as he talked.

"The tanker? Right now she has just about eighty-one hundred gallons of gasoline. It varies sometimes with destination, but I usually carry the better part of ten thousand gallons."

"Boy, that would make one helluva bonfire!"

The driver wasn't nearly as excited by the notion and shivered it off.

"You ain't just whistling Dixie ... "

The morning overcast was getting thicker, with less time for the sun to find its way through the clouds. It looked like it might rain on everyone's parade after all. And there was hardly a soul who wanted it to go that way.

The parents hoped for sunshine, to distract their children, and all the children wished for their happy outing that involved astronauts. The parade members and band would much rather it stay sunny. They would have to march anyway, in their shined shoes; feathers plumed and spit shined instruments, whose luster could only be appreciated in the sun. And who wouldn't rather walk in the warm sun than slog through puddles and compete with thunder?

The police officers were determined that it should not rain. Even though fewer would turn out for the parade, thus making the crowds easier to handle in the park, it would be a totally different story once everyone made their way to their cars and tried to exit. The inclement weather would add to accidents and problems to an already rushed and agitated traffic situations, and probably add hours to the delay.

The Mayor had taken the possibility of rain into account, and had arranged, through one of his staff members' brother in law who managed one of the more luxurious hotels of the town, for several adjoining rooms on the top floor be reserved for ceremonies – large enough for the astronauts, the Mayor and city officials, the press and a few select citizens, important members of groups and organizations. He had arranged for food, drink and other niceties to appease the appetites and afford comforts to those involved, should the rain try to spoil their affair.

The sniper, if his thoughts were said aloud, would also prefer a sunny day. Visibility would be excellent, the wind would not be a factor, nor would he have to worry about the rain affecting his shot or weapon. Sunshine definitely would make his job easier. And besides, everyone loves a sunny day.

CHAPTER ELEVEN

The roof was quiet compared to the noise coming from the streets below as the people made ready for the parade. Every space on the curbs was being filled with strollers, blankets, even lounge chairs. Everyone wanted a good view of the spectacular event. Alone on the roof, the sniper reviewed his course of action.

"Let's see. The parade will start at this point ... " He was looking again at the map, which by this time was beginning to show wear from constant use. " ... after about three or four marching bands, the astronauts will make their debut – no doubt in an open car, since the sun is shining ... then they'll come around the corner and up this street until they come to the intersection --- here – turn up this block, then a little better than half-way down the block they'll take a right up the driveway into the park to the speakers' stands which will be on the grass about here. The good Mayor should stand right about here and the bands will probably set up to the right of the Mayor's seat ... and the 'nauts will be the last to go up the stand to the roaring crowd – probably to sit on his left ... right about here."

The man continued over his plan, away from the bustle on the streets below. If the masses had put as much thought into figuring out where and when everything would take place, they may have chosen their own seats differently.

"Now, most of the people will congregate right around the front of the speakers' stand, and if my measurements are accurate, that is a distance of about six hundred and fifty yards." He glanced from the map to the park below, gauging his thoughts against reality as he spoke to himself, recognizing the distance and the feel as he held his rifle close.

"I'll be shooting down at an angle of about thirty-five degrees ... " as he was setting his rifle's scope to the soft clicks "just ... about ... right ... " and then moved cautiously to the edge of the roof, looking through his sights at the people moving below. After a minor adjustment, he put the weapon down, and looked for a moment at the crowd.

"They look pretty down there ... from this far away, you just see the colors of their clothes; the blues, the reds, golds, whites ... from this distance you can't see their selfish actions and egotistical thoughts. Just a bunch of well-dressed ants – hurrying back and forth without any real meaning, bouncing off one another in their excitement. That's the problem with these little bastards, they don't think they're 'bad' people, just too much in a hurry to stop and think ... so because they don't think – time, feelings, sometimes even life is wasted in a single careless moment ... and no one is to blame.

"That's the problem. They don't think they are responsible because they weren't thinking, like it is a valid excuse. They wave it high in the air as their flag. That's why big money bosses run this country – not because they are actually smarter – but because they don't mind thinking a little, and they just think about their own interests. No more selfish, no more intelligent, just don't mind working a little harder to screw each other over. Not any different at all. There is no craft or skill, just a drive for selfish perpetuation ... and for that ... they are equally damned."

The people down on the street were, in fact, jostling one another back and forth as they made their way through the crowds, but it was expected, and no one seemed to mind; maybe even added to the excitement of the day. The parade had started on time and the people merged even closer together, to act as one huge multicolored wave moving towards the astronauts' car as it slowly moved in front of them, then slowly moved down the street. The mass of people would start to swell and come tumbling forward, inundating the police, moving the line closer to the passing celebrities. From a bird's eye view, it looked like a scene at the beach, with the people and police moving back and forth, rising and ebbing like the waves of the ocean on the sand.

Half the parade passed the intersection before the leaders entered the park and made their way toward the speakers' stand. The Mayor and astronauts attempted to organize themselves for the bands to pass the stand in review. The sniper was getting set as well, although his priming and primping was of a much more serious nature.

He meticulously started to lay out his spare clips of ammunition, the ammo he carefully selected like the finest of vintage wines. His selection was regardless of the name on the boxes, as it was unimportant, but the power and worth of the bullet, only a marksman would understand and appreciate. The bullet was a 308 magnum. It had the same length as the 30-06 cartridge, thus fitting into his rifle with only minor modifications to the extractor. Flying at such high velocities, the bullet is extremely deadly, and has been known to take down charging bears at up to 500 yards. Weighing only 180 grams, or 1/3 of an ounce, the bullet's real worth was in its fine expanding qualities – mushrooming to more than three times its original diameter once impact.

After the sniper laid out his ammunition he began checking his specially prepared scope mounted on the left side of the receiver to permit clip-loading and top ejection. He then loaded the weapon and adjusted the scope with the full load in the rifle. Down below, the end of the parade was in view.

Most of the band had passed to the right of the stand, and the remaining dignitaries were moving out of their cars and climbing the few steps to take their places. As the last of the parade passed, the Mayor, astronauts and city officials began arranging themselves for the speeches. The crowds were already settling around the stand and those who did not wish to stay for the "talks" had begun to shuffle out, pushing and excusing themselves through the throng.

The Mayor had already stepped to the microphone to introduce the astronauts, say a few words in their praise and present them with a key to the city along with a few other accolades of honor. The ceremony was brief and to the point, the astronauts' remarks were as brief as the Mayor's, and the remaining dignitaries merely smiled and cheered politely with the crowd. The band played the national anthem, a few in the crowd sang along, and the ceremonies were concluded.

The Mayor rose, as did the astronauts and the officials, and began to move at a leisurely pace toward the waiting cars. Reporters crowded around them firing pictures and talking over one another. The band members busied themselves putting away their instruments and conversing while the crowd was in the normal confusion that follows the end of a public gathering involving a couple thousand people leaving to go back to their own individual thousands of lives.

A man, clutching a little girl by the hand so they would not be separated in the moving mass, uttered a scream and fell over. The little girl stopped motionless but the cry was indistinguishable in the rumble of the crowd. Only a few noticed the man fall, wondering if he had suffered a sudden heart-attack. A loud bang was thought to have been heard when an elderly lady, moving slowly through the crowd with her son and his family, fell to the ground clutching her chest. A younger woman who had been complaining to her boyfriend that the wind was blowing and messing her hair, literally had her head explode with the next breeze onto him and passerby. People now began to scream as the panic spread ... a realization of the horror that was happening.

The Mayor looked around, reacting to the individual scream: "What the hell is going on here?" He did not hear his own possible answers, for at the moment he was realizing that there was something going on, his ability to think of answers was ripped apart by a piercing bullet carefully aimed from the roof.

One man, and then several others in the crowd, looked in the direction of the distant hotel roof, as the terror spread. The people were going mad with fear. The sniper had stuck and death was falling all over.

"Will ya look at 'em run. Out of all the firefights and bloodshed I have seen, never did I imagine what firing into a bunch of selfish brainless asses would be like. Run you little bastards, run ... but you aren't going to get away, not today." He aimed again and fired.

A policeman crawled to the speakers' stand that was knocked over, grabbed the microphone, which was miraculously still on, crouched behind the steps and ordered everyone to drop. "Find any cover at all, just get down and stay down!" He could see the horror on the faces as they tried to cope with the events. Some people had enough composure to listen and hide, some into the cars that were parked close by, some in buildings; most just kept on running, seemingly in circles, unable to escape. The area was clearing however, of the living ... .leaving only contorted bodies of the dead and dying strewn over the green park grass.

The policeman at the microphone surveyed the area, paused a moment, deciding whether to speak again, deciding against it and placed the mike on the ground. He carefully crawled to the cover of a cruiser parked near the edge of the grass. His men had done a fairly good job of clearing the area, although little could be done to calm the panic. The firing did not come as fast as it had before, and sirens filled the air as ambulances rushed to the scene. The attendants teamed up with the police officer before trying to reach the wounded victims. Even though a great deal of caution was used, a few of the CMTs were shot. Many of the victims crawled over to waiting stretchers, desperately trying to reach the safety of the ambulance before it was too late.

Only minutes had passed since the first shot had been fired, and actually less time than that since the chaos of reality set in, but it had seemed like it had been an eternity to everyone but the sniper, and there was still no end in sight. Now the firing had almost ceased entirely and full ambulances were racing toward area hospitals.

Every hospital has standard operating procedure should certain situations and contexts arise. These only go into effect when the given disaster presents itself, usually with a specific code being announced over the page system to alert all hospital personnel, but to minimize alarming the patients. "Doctor Christopher ... Cycle II, Doctor Christopher, Cycle II" alerted the staff to a riot situation in this particular hospital.

Student nurses, faculty members, LPNs and other staff members not assigned a specific area will meet in the Nursing Services Office. Most areas have a call list of personnel not on duty and usually as many as possible will report to the hospital to help in any way they can, swiping their card to get in like a normal day. Visitors trying to enter the building will be asked to return tomorrow and all non-emergency departments will be on standby to lend any assistance possible. The main entry handles any inevitable overflow from the emergency room and male aids from all floors bring any available stretchers to both areas. The nursing staff organizes supplies for immediate aid to the injured. All available doctors, interns and residents report to be ready when victims arrive. The drills, and there had been more than one, now seemed a distant memory to many of the staff.

The emergency room complex covered the left side of the hospital building, with second entrance for emergency vehicles only, and a rear exit door where corpses are taken out. As you enter the complex through the main entrance, before the swinging doors, there is a waiting room for relatives and friends of patients. Once beyond the doors, there is another reception desk and a number of treatment rooms branching off on both corridors. Right now, people are everywhere.

"What the hell is going on – what on earth happened?!?" The doctor turned an unbelievable expression toward the closest nurse who was checking the bandage supply closet.

"Well, doctor ... it's like World War III happened right around the corner somewhere. The ambulances just began pouring in all these victims, rolling one after another ... "

The nurse's sorrow filled explanation was cut short by the doctor as he saw a more accurate source and began making his way through the mess of people; a policeman had emerged through the side entrance helping a lady with blood smeared on her face.

"For God's sake – what happened?"

The policeman let the woman go into the hands of a nurse and tried to straighten up. His uniform was disheveled and his mind was a wreck. His pride wanted to care about his appearance but somewhere in his mind he knew what we all know and hope to never see. When real danger calls, the real heroes step forth, and everyone else just has to tuck in their shirt after they've run to safety, if they've made it. He was standing there now, so all that was left to tell was the story. He sighed off his pride and struggled through the tears welled by the insanity of it all.

"It was right after the parade, doc – the ceremony for the astronauts, you know, the one at the park today ... some nut opened up with a rifle, shooting into the crowd ... men, women, children, old ladies ... I'd say twenty dead, fifty hurt ... by now, there's probably fifty more hurt. Things are a real mess out there ... everybody's yelling and screaming ... it's a real mess ... "

The policeman stopped at the door of the room as the curtain was drawn around the woman he came in with. He didn't want to leave and go back out into it all. The doctor, who had been looking around the room at the chaos that was tumbling in, trying to organize it, making sense of how it all happened and what he was going to do to make it ordered again, turned toward the police officer. He wasn't more than 25 years old, probably on the streets of the force for a few years. This was way too much for anyone to handle – never mind a boy. As if the police officer heard the doc's thoughts, he mustered his courage, turned and headed toward the exit ... back to his car with the engine still running.

"Alright – nurse, see which surgeons are available and make sure the off-duty ones have been called in ... see how many operating rooms have been readied and which ones can be made ready – it looks like we are going to need everything we've got."

The doctor looked up and spoke through all the disorder that surrounded him, as if with a sonar or high pitch sound only heard by those that worked there, and the rest of the people seemed to continue in the chaos.

"The rest of you – remind everyone to check for ID bracelets, cards, anything pertaining to specific allergies, diabetes, etc. ... we have enough going on that we don't need any more to take care of. Let's avoid any mistakes if possible I want everyone blood-typed right away ... and we'll handle the less serious wounds down here and everyone else will get prepped for upstairs ... DOA's hold in the patient department until everything else gets taken care of."

CHAPTER TWELVE

Up on the roof, all was quiet. The sniper had stopped firing for the time being, and was watching the chaos he had created through his scope. The police were still aiding the wounded and cleaning up the mess. No one of any consequence had seen which roof the firing had come from, and since the shooting had stopped, the police were going to have to search all logical buildings in the area, giving the sniper plenty of time to escape, if and when he chose to. For the moment, he turned his attention to the adjacent streets where the crowds were still running.

"Those people are really scared – look at 'em stomping over one another to get away ... terrified! Put a little fear in their hearts ... " He stopped in his analysis as he caught sight of a new menace. "And what do we have here ... a tanker?"

He held his scope ready, gazing hard at the red tanker parked on the side of the street. The hood was raised, and the cab was pulled practically onto the sidewalk. The driver was in the driver's seat playing with the controls, completely unaware of what was going on around him.

"Well, what do ya know? Now that would make one helluva bonfire ... let's see ... " His mind starts searching for the correct answers as he reaches over for his pack of things. He pulls out a box of tracer shells, and lets experience take over.

"First, eject all the rounds in the weapon, put in five rounds of tracers, and then three regular rounds ... " It's like a seminar on how to blow up tankers, and the teacher is going to do a live demonstration to finish the lecture. His fingers followed through the actions like programmed automatons, agile and sure.

"Now, to the tanker. First, we open her up ... "The sniper sights and then fires at the truck in the middle of the tanker about two feet from the bottom, just at the curve of the body. Three holes appear in quick succession, in line, each about the size of a silver dollar, immediately releasing streams of gasoline to fall freely on the ground. The truck driver, who had remained in the cab throughout the day, waiting for the repair man to show, heard the bullets hit the truck. He hesitated, weighing the danger of leaving the safety of the cab, then got out to investigate.

After stepping down from the cab, he moved to the side of the truck and caught sight of the gasoline pooling up. He started to walk hurriedly toward the hole, casting thought aside, until the sense of danger to the people hurrying down the street in panic hit him.

Up on the roof, the sniper adjusted his aim for the final time in preparation, and fired the remaining rounds in the rifle ... the five rounds of tracer bullets. Three went smashing into the trailer; one went through the fleshy part of the driver's leg and then ate its way into the gasoline tank of the truck; the final shot was aimed at the puddle of gasoline accumulated on the ground.

In the first seconds, nothing seemed to happen, with the exception of the driver spinning to the ground and trying desperately to crawl away. The people who had chosen this particular street as their escape route kept right on running, taking no notice of the fallen driver. Then with a bright flash and a loud "VROOM" the tanker split down the side and the top lifted off. Bright orange flames came pouring out onto the street. The heat was so intense that the body of the trailer began to melt as the flames engulfed the truck. The wounded driver who managed to crawl as far as the front of the cab was rocketed by the blast. He looked up in time to see the eight thousand one hundred gallons of gasoline come bursting from the split tanker, on its way to consume him. Those who were running alongside or near the truck when it was absorbed into the fiery holocaust went up like little sticks of greased candles. They were incinerated in a matter of moments, the screams of anguish seeming to come after the fact.

The tidal wave of fiery gasoline swept down the street from curb to curb. Those who managed to escape the fire of the sniper now ran to escape, but all to no avail. The heat from the wave was so intense that the street lights along the edge of the sidewalk shattered and the poles began to curve as they melted.

The sniper saw almost with amusement as one man, a late leaver of the scene as he had been hiding underneath a parked car and just now judged it safe to leave, raced around the corner of the street and saw the wave of flames about twenty-five feet away and moving toward him. He stopped, stared, eyes bugging out as he saw the unfortunate victims, screaming, burning, running. He whirled around, gave a little jump in the air, and ran screaming back around the corner as if all the devils in hell were after him. He was saved. For the people caught in this ground zero, there was no escape, nor rescue. Sixty-three people are gone ... and the roof is quiet again.

Across town, the fire station had no idea of the bedlam that is taking place, and they sit and talk on a breezy day that ended with no rain. "So I said to the chief – 'Chief, I am not going to wear that goddamn bunker coat – it's about as fireproof as my kid's pajamas for Christ's ... " His humorous banter is cut into by the overhead speakers.

"ATTENTION – ENGINES ten, eight, seven ... LADDER two ... RESCUE UNITS two and four ... and FOAM TRUCK ... Gasoline fire on west of park – signal twenty-three ... Caution Advised – there is a sniper reported in the vicinity ... time out."

Immediately, the station is a clatter of noise and regulated confusion. Men caught eating drop everything; men in the middle of dreams are up in seconds; everyone rushing to their stations. They board the truck in practice time and are on the road before they have a chance to reflect upon the loudspeaker's message: the concept of fighting a treacherous fire, with a trained gunman who is obviously a madman as well.

The men look to the Chief for that comforting word, but this isn't something he handles every day, either. In all his 27 years, he never had to do anything like this. It's like going down to a war-zone, with all its chaos, danger and death. He turned his head to the driver, away from the looks of all his men, and patted him on the shoulder through his thick coat, "Let's get this thing moving ... " and then turned back to his crew, mustered up every ounce of faith he had. This wasn't going to be a firefight and everyone knew it. "Get sharp ... this one's going to be a regular bastard."

The trucks – high, huge monsters – were being revved up as the firemen jumped onto their backs, then like stallions they are off to the races. They all have 12-cylinder engines with dual ignition systems, so if one fails the engine will still start. The pumps in the truck can shoot sixty gallons per minute.

As the trucks approached the fire, black smoke and huge flames could be seen. It took the engines four minutes and twenty seconds to get there and by this time, the fire had spread to the buildings lined on one side of the street. The gasoline had soaked into the pavement, the grass, and the bottom levels of the buildings. The flames seemed to engulf the entire block.

Engines ten and eight immediately laid four lines, using hydrants almost a block away since all the hydrants on this block were inaccessible due to flames. Precious seconds went by as the firefighters moved to hook up the water lines. Three of the men scanned the adjoining streets for any victims who had escaped the flames, but were in need of help. They found no one. Engine seven set up at the opposite end of the street and after laying their lines, began pouring water on the blaze. The two foam trucks centered their attack closest to the gasoline truck itself. The foam, once applied to the gasoline, floated on top of the gasoline and formed a vapor lock, cutting off the oxygen from the fire, in theory. It seemed like the flames rose higher, the buildings adding fuel to an overfed fire.

The battalion chief arrived and immediately requested engines five, nine and ladder one be dispatched to the scene. The engines were to give extra hose to the newly arrived engines. Hydrants from
as ... ked up and relays formed. All the
fire ... r packs to reduce the
sm ... o be a long fight, and
th

... ity of the blaze, arrived
w ... d post and requested
e ... d along with two more
fo ... the buildings from the
s ... ings were precariously
c ... were empty of people,
s ... ny feeble rescues in the
f

Within a half hour of the explosion, a staff headquarters had been set up at the central fire station, and over one hundred and ten off duty firefighters reported for duty. The electric and gas companies were directed to shut down all lines leading into the area, and hundreds of thousands of gallons of water had been pumped into the fire. By the time the fire was felt to be contained, ambulances had already begun running injured firefighters to the hospital, the Salvation Army and Red Cross. Operators of heavy equipment had offered their services and the police had successfully blockaded the entire area, keeping unsuspecting spectators away.

The scene of the fire now could have been the setting for the end of the world. Confusion and exhaustion appeared everywhere as ambulance EMTs, policemen and firefighters rushed about to help wherever it was needed, running ceaselessly through the maze of disorder. The buildings began to smolder where the flames were squelched, while the street itself for the most part was still a boiling, fiery path of flames. The screams of the sirens, the pounding of the water and the incessant roar of the fire, added the final touch of illusion to the very real scene.

The sniper looked at his watch. It had only been forty-five minutes and thirty-two seconds. From the first shot at the truck 'til now. Three quarters of an hour up here – an eternity, down there.

"Man, princess would really be proud of me now. Those people are really hurting. They are a bunch of sorry asses, for sure. RUN, run, you S.O.B.'s., but there's no place for you to hide. The blaze was sweeping to a side street, while ambulances were still removing victims from the park. Sirens filled the city as the fire trucks made their way to the park. The sniper moved quietly about on the roof, elated at moments as he watched the stricken crowds, serious at the next as he considered his next course of action, always remembering his position on the roof, constantly checking each side of the building for fear of being flanked. He scanned the area and saw nothing. "That fire is going to keep them busy for hours ... "

As he turned to go back to his post, he unconsciously, pure habit, pulled back the bolt on his rifle, causing the expended shell to eject. The ejected shell flew through the air, hitting a wire, landing on the edge of the roof, spinning in the wind. Below, on the quiet street, came the echo of the footsteps of the beat cop.

"Everything is so quiet over here ... I guess I'm not sorry I'm missing the hell that's going on over there ... not much I could do if I was there anyway, I guess .... .that fire is sure a mess ... Anyway, I'll keep my eyes open ... Portable Four Out."

He stopped to put his "squawk" box away, and started to walk on. At that precise moment, the shell spinning and wavering in the wind on the ledge fell down. It hit the sidewalk and bounced noisily in back of the policeman. He turned at the sound and began to walk back a few steps. Now time becomes immobile as the gods weigh their decision. Just as the policeman was in the process of turning around, the wind swept a scrap of paper lying on the ground. The wind died, and the paper settled over the shell. The rookie cop scanned the sidewalk, seeing nothing. He listened for a moment ... heard nothing and continued on his beat. Just as he turned to leave, the wind blew the paper away. The shell, now naked, lay at his feet.

At the same moment, a few of the horrified crowd came racing down the street toward him. His attention drawn away, he started to move toward them. They turned up a side street, but not before his shoe hit the shell on the street. He bent down and picked it up.

Holding the shell in his hand, he looked around. The abandoned hotel in front of him was the only building within a reasonable distance. He looked at the shell again, and at the deserted building.

His mind now raced far ahead of his footsteps as he moved toward the front.

"Perhaps the sniper is in the building right now ... maybe he already saw me pick up the shell ... maybe he was here and already left ... escaped right out from under my nose ... "

He pushed open the old front door, and stepped into the gloomy lobby. The musty smell hit him right away, and the debris on the floor speaks of years of disuse. As he walked ahead, he kept glancing over his shoulder. He noticed the marks his footsteps were leaving. About ten feet to the left where he was walking in, in the dim light he was able to make out another set of marks. Slowly he pulled out his communicator.

"Portable four to headquarters ... Portable four to headquarters ... come in ... "

"This is headquarters to portable four, headquarters to portable four ... go ahead."

"This is portable four ... I have entered a seven-story deserted building – looks like it used to be a hotel ... pretty dark and dusty in here ... upon entering I noticed footprints on the floor, more than one set of tracks here, but one set is very recent ... " He constantly glanced over his shoulders and into the shadows. From what was described to him about what went on at the park, they were dealing with a serious animal, who didn't have one care about killing you. " ... outside the building I found a spent shell that appears to have fallen from the roof ... this may be the place where the sniper is shooting from ... the most recent set of prints lead to the end of the lobby, near the elevators to a door marked 'exit' ... looks like it probably is the stairway to the roof ... he must have used the stairway. I think we'll need the special squad to handle this one ... you'd better send three or four other black and whites for backups, and for blocking off the intersections ... "

"Copy that, portable four. The special team is already assembled and will be ready to move into the area shortly. You just saved a lot of search time, portable four. We recommend you backtrack or stay put ... "

"This is portable four ... acknowledged and out ... "

The policeman, tense and cautious, wiped his hand across his forehead. The beads of sweat moistened his hand. He looked around for a place to wait, somewhere he could watch the door and at the same time not be seen, should the sniper decide to leave by the same door. He finally settled in the corner opposite the door behind an old overstuffed couch. "Just have to wait until they get here ... "

At the police headquarters, the captain addressed a group of eight men in an empty room in the back of the station. "All right you men, we have the probable location of the sniper ... " he pointed to a building on a map on a projection screen. "You will take orders from the unit commander once you reach the destination ... now hustle."

The small squad moved quickly out of the station and into their van. They shuffled into the back and swung the doors shut. The unmarked van took off at a ridiculous speed and didn't slow down the whole way. The men in the back who had more courage than most, made small talk about it.

"Man, this guy should learn to hold the curves better."

The lightweight van took the next one at fifty-five and the men hung on the rails again. Another one of the men smiled.

"Why take your time to get killed, might as well hurry up, why wait."

A third of the men chimed in now – it seemed the excitement of the situation was forcing humor.

"We have to hurry up and give the sniper a chance to shoot at us. Criminals have rights too, you know."

The unit commander took his turn to speak out to the eight, but there was no humor and he was only speaking as it was pertinent to the situation.

"Listen up ... all those who have automatic sidearm and would like to use the standard revolver – if you feel you would be more proficient, can do so ... "There was an admonishing tone to his voice. This was more serious than anything his team had handled. They had no idea how many men were on the roof, what kind of training or weaponry they had, the building itself was of unknown status and could have been rigged six ways from Sunday. All they knew was they were dealing with professionals and that intent to kill was present.

The van took one more sharp turn and came to a screeching halt, then slowly crept down the street to the hotel where the sniper was thought to be holed up on the roof. They were the Special Police Force Unit. Their equipment consists of a transceiver radio, seven by fifty binoculars, automatic sidearm, shoulder auto weapon and ballistic helmet. The vehicle carries optional equipment, including a lightweight aluminum body armor for each officer, tear gas grenades and launching equipment, gas masks, cover smoke grenades, signal flares, shields, infrared and sniper scopes, and a host of other essentials. Their clothing consisted of dark cover-all type one-piece outfit. Helmet shields and equipment worn on the body or hand carried were also in a matching dark color. They wear rubber, waffle airborne boots. All insignia, glistening objects on belts, shoulders and so forth are non-existent.

It started as a group of volunteers – ten men to the squad. They were to receive an extra fifty dollars a month compensation to take on the more dangerous tasks that the force would face. The suggestion of being qualified in all types of weaponry, expert marksman, trained in first aid, mountaineering and in-fighting had become more of a requirement. The ten was now down to four and they are the elite in police work. Not many cities can afford this squad, or perhaps, need this squad.

CHAPTER THIRTEEN

The vehicle rolled to a stop, and the men emerged from the back cautiously but with speed, the sniper could be aware of their arrival and already have them in his scope. The unit commander immediately takes charge and starts to give status and orders.

"As far as we know, he's on that roof over there, just beyond this wall; the building is by itself on the corner. Now the boys in blue have all these streets blocked off, but I'm calling for a three-quarter blockade – we don't know what we're dealing with here. If it's just one man, he's good – too good. We have our own sharpshooters, and if anything shows up on the edge of that roof, they'll keep him down."

He paused and looked up at the building, seeing through their cover, imagining the sniper, barely visible, taking a shot at himself or his men as they made their way to the building.

"Keep in mind, he has armor piercing rounds, so he doesn't need a head shot. No heroics ... if a man falls ... leave him. No sense in two widows. Do I make myself clear?" The men all continued to ready themselves, equipping their "bullet proof" vests, despite their probable insignificance. "We'll need tear gas, three each, and masks."

The men gathered their own equipment. They were tense now and the joking had stopped. The adrenaline rushing through each of them made their hearts beat faster and respiration accelerate. They were ready. They moved out suspiciously toward the building, eyes always on the roof.

No shots were fired. Fortunately for them, the sniper was preoccupied – eating. He was stationed behind the wall that housed the door leading from the roof. Presently he finished his sandwich and began his rounds, checking the perimeter, contemplating a possible escape, when darkness fell. He cautiously put his head up over the edge of the front of the building, just in time to see the last officer disappear below, beyond his line of vision.

He turned back to the roof and sat with his back against the weathered brick edge.

"They finally spotted me ... Damn! Looks like the trial is over and jury will deliver the verdict soon. Well, they'll get their money's worth ... " He looked up into the sky and noticed a chopper, hanging in the polluted air above the city about a mile away. "Yessir, they definitely have me in a bind ... by a small margin ... about four or five thousand to one."

Once inside the musty hotel, the small group of men re-organized quickly and received their instructions. With only a passing nod of acknowledgment to the rookie police officer in the lobby, they immediately set about getting ready for the climb to the roof. The commander spoke calmly and quietly.

"Alright, our chopper pilot said the sniper spotted us about two minutes ago ... we have one tango on the roof ... keep close to the wall, we don't know if he's alone. Everyone put on their masks – we'll hit him with the tear gas first. He knows we are here."

The rest of the men were silent as they started up the seven flights of stairs. The sniper, already alert, turned to the sound of movement, and sensed them, rather than saw them coming.

"Looks like they're moving down there ... they're probably going to send someone up here to see what the lay of the land is ... " He moved inside the heavy metal door to the head of the stairs, then silently into the hallway, working to a point that looked right down the stairwell. The four men moving through the hallways and up the stairs were using the natural light to find their way, which was dim at its most bright.

The lead man reached the top few steps, did not see the string across the stairs, nor did he see the stick that was attached to it some four feet away, hidden by the railing. Nor could he have known that it was rigged to a trap door in the ceiling which was aching to release the 200 pounds of rock and rubble that the sniper had placed there – indeed placed with care, having strategically placed long nails sticking out weighed down by the deadfall rocks.

The men in the lobby were beginning to feel the high tension just as the chopper pilot rang in. "This is chopper three to unit commander ... the damn guy ran inside the building, been in there three, maybe four minutes ... he knows something is up ... may be a trap ... better warn those men going up ... "

The unit commander knew this guy was good, and after seeing the footprints for himself, he knew he was alone. He didn't want to believe that one person was capable of all this carnage; not because it was too evil, but to be that damn accurate and efficient ... "all we need is an ambush," he thought. He immediately switched on the transceiver, opening communication with the group.

" ... This is unit one ... shit you guys ... no time ... get out of there now ... he's wise, may be a trap ... "

The men on the steps received the message and froze. Then slowly the weapons came up to firing level, and they began backpedaling down the stairs, but the sniper was wise, and had heard the crackling com and decided to strike. He leaped out, letting out a yell that echoed through the hallway, then put four shots down the stairwell. The men caught in the act of checking behind them were totally open. The lead man, still on the precarious step, turned to the shots, and caught the trip wire string on his boot. The stick fell and the rocks and gravel came smashing down from the other side of the trap door, nails and all.

The spikes that were stuck in the door may have appeared to be in a haphazard manner but were placed so that one of them hit the target about neck level. As the door fell, the spike struck, entering the back of the neck, slipping through muscle and tissue and ending with a ripping of the carotid artery, causing massive internal bleeding coupled with a small slushy yell. The rest of the group fell back and reached the bottom of the stairs and flung themselves around the corner.

They staggered out into the somewhat brighter light of the dim lobby, gasping. The unit commander accosted them. "What the hell happened up there?" His hope of the men getting the sniper was being drowned out by the slow recognition of the shock on the faces of the survivors. After a moment more of breathing, one of the remaining men spoke.

"Get him? We never even saw the son of a bitch. The place was booby trapped. We were almost to the top of the ceiling when it literally fell on us. Our point man is down ... hit bad, real bad ... "

The unit commander listened intently. They had to keep the sniper out on the roof if they wanted any chance of getting up that stairwell.

"We'll gas the whole stairwell. That will keep him out on the roof ... the chopper can keep an eye on him ... let us know if he decides to come back in ... use all your tear gas."

This idea of semi-crippling the offender first, brought new life to the men. With little hesitation they reached for their canisters and started up the stairs again. Half way up, the gas was released. Then the men, protected by their masks, began the long tense climb to the top. The gas wound its way up the stairwell, seeping into every nook and cranny, every crack in the wall in the old building. The chopper notified the unit commander that the mist had reached the top and was beginning to seep out onto the roof. The unit commander relayed the message to his men. This time, there would be no lack of precaution, no underestimation, no mistakes.

The two lead men came up the last flight of stairs, firing steadily, giving the sniper no chance to move inside the stairwell.

The sniper had no intention of moving to the roof, but went back to the stairwell into an apartment he had prepared for such an emergency.

The heat, the smoke and smell from tear gas and cordite filled the air. A small fog started to fill the upper floors. The noise ... intense, the sweat running from his body in rivulets. His anger is visible. Inside he is scared but he does not give in, for to give in is to die and he has come too far to do that. The police are getting closer and closer. Bullets snapping through the air hitting walls thunking into doors, wood fragmenting and flying all over like little pieces of shrapnel. He was screaming and yelling, shooting back. Time to go – his window of opportunity now – he went.

In some of those old apartments in New York, especially the one he chose, there were dumbwaiters, little box like elevators that went down to the basement for the carrying of laundry, food, whatever needed to be moved. He had secured a rope from this apartment that fed all the way to the basement. At the time, moments away, he was going to shimmy down the rope, with the aid of some climbing gloves that were attached to his belt, to the safety of that old basement with its familiar musty smell and odor of coal.

NOW, NOW. GO, GO!

He wormed his way to the front door at this point pretty well shot to pieces, took two grenades, pulled the pins and threw them out the door. He could hear them bounce down the hallway and then explode. Two large bangs. More screaming and yelling.

He made his way back into the apartment through the living room, into the kitchen to the dumbwaiter. He grabbed his gloves and let himself down feet first holding tightly onto the rope. He started out slowly and kept himself slightly bent, stopping or slowing down as needed by resting on the ledges of different floors that the dumbwaiter hit. Halfway down, he had planted a couple of grenades with a trip wire leading from them to the ground. As his body hit the basement floor – he grabbed the wires, moved several feet away and pulled the wires – several seconds later, two explosions effectively cutting off anyone from following him down.

Now also in this complex, every building was joined by tunnels so that in bad weather residents could move easily from one building to another. He broke the calumine sticks which lit the way. He could still hear the firing upstairs which meant they hadn't missed him ... yet.

As he moved through the tunnels, the noise became faint and then nonexistent as he reached the last building. He then made his way out onto the street he had chosen which was several blocks away from the shooting and fire he had started with the gasoline truck. The black plume of smoke undulating into the air and the screaming of emergency vehicles was very quiet.

Among the several cars parked along the curb was a blue Toyota. He dusted himself off as well as he could, put his PPK into his pocket and walked casually over to the car. Put the key into the lock, opened the door, got in. He started the car and carefully and slowly drove away. As he pulled away – the scene in the rear view mirror was chaotic with lights and smoke. The view receded. He realized he was free ... free.

He smiled.

PART II

2011 AD

CHAPTER FOURTEEN

It was a hot, hot day. The kind of day that the air temperature reads 98°, the heat index 104°, and the pavement hit a high of 114°. The kind of day that the minute you stepped out of the cold protection of your house, your shirt stuck to you like a paper mache mask to your face.

Frank, through the years, and shirt style after shirt style, found the best one for him was the polo shirt. Open at the neck to breathe, a collar to receive the sweat and a definite must, a pocket to carry his reading glasses.

The kind of day that as you walked to the mailbox, you had to squint your eyes to keep out the harsh glare of the sun.

He walked a little slower now, which happened when he retired from the active life. The days at the trade school on the Hudson and the many different posts, Vietnam among them, included meeting many different people and making many acquaintances and a few good friends. Connections and power from any and all associations were kept and maintained. Going into the private sector after Harvard B School meant the cycle started all over. He loved it.

Retirement seemed to arrive out of the blue; he left, but luckily he was liked, had his buddies, connections and respect. So much so, that now and then they came to him for advice, counsel and opinions based on his years of expertise and knowledge. It was good to feel wanted.

He reached the mailbox and pulled out the solitary letter. It looked a little worn from wear and the postmark was a week old. It looked like it came from maybe South America. Maybe one of his friends, he had them from all over. He looked again at the letter and the hairs on the back of his neck stood out.

It couldn't be – not after all this time. What was it – thirty-four years? He walked a little quicker to the house, went into his den, sat down at his desk, looked at the letter again. "My God, it can't be, but maybe it's about time," he thought as he reached for his bayonet letter opener. He inserted it carefully into the envelope and slowly opened the letter. It was a mixture of writing and printing. The greeting the same old bombastic style. "Frank, salutations and felicitations." It was him, his brother who he had helped thirty-four years ago, and to this day had never written or been heard from since.

He took the letter, arranged the pages, put on his exhaust fan, selected a cigar, clipped it, lit it, moved to a comfortable position and started to read.

"Dear Frank, salutations and felicitations. I know, I know, it's been a long time – more than I care to remember. I've been down here where it's been quiet and peaceful. I've had my hand in a couple of dealings, but nothing to write home about. I am in great health and want to thank you for the aid you gave me. Those killings are in the past, a necessary evil. It's over – gone into the mists of time. As far away as Alice is. I accept the inevitability of the situation. It's over for me, and I am coming home. No one ever knew who I was, maybe suspected but never knew. So I am coming back to live a normal quiet life. I love you and thank you. We will get together when I get back. Love ya, Louis."

Frank put down the letter, walked, poured himself a Frau Angelica, went back to the desk, put the phone on quick dial. "He's back, sounds good and healthy. When he comes to see me, we can get him."

The day dark, the rain coming down very wet and sticky, the thunder loud and rumbling, the lightning very bright and static. The green house on the small hill would glow dark and light as the storm continued. Louis moved quietly around the house blending into the shadows. He noticed the setting of the house – white double garage door, the house facing west with a plain simple front lined by bushes with three palm trees. The back had a screened in pool which looked comfortable. Cars were parked on the street and on aprons – no telling friend or foe. But hell he was visiting his brother – who would care he was here and who would know? He rang the bell.

Frank opened the door. He stood for a moment, looked Louis up and down, grabbed him and gave him a hug. Kissed his cheek. Louis returned the hug and felt glad to be back.

"Damn, Louis, you look good. A little older but still the same half-smile."

"Well, you didn't change too much. Still slender, with that little mustache and close haircut. I think the more things change the more they stay the same."

"Come in, come in." Louis walked into the small foyer which was tiled in a light brown parchment like marble with a small, unpretentious chandelier hanging overhead.

"Here, have a seat in the living room, or as we say down here, the great room –"

"Looks pretty good," observed Louis as he took in the leather chairs and couch. "Say isn't that Aunt Kimmie's couch?"

"You got it. When she passed I took that, and several other pieces of furniture from Pop and Mom's house and Nona's. It makes for a comfortable setting, don't you think?"

"Yes it does." Louis sat down.

"What do you want to drink?"

"Just a cold glass of water unless you have Pena water."

"I do," Frank replied, "one of the things Cathy liked which I grew accustomed to."

Cathy, Frank's wife, had died of cancer several years before. They had been close.

"I know what you mean, Frank. I am that way about Alice, kept a few things close to me when she died, but anyway back to the present. I'm here, you're here so let's talk future – and the way I can fit in."

Frank came over and sat down facing Louis. He looked serious.

"You know Lou, when you left there was quite a mess – people dead left and right. Rumors all over." He took a sip. "Nothing anyone could prove. The police and a couple of Federal agencies came close, but I, through a couple of associates, pulled some strings that put them off the track."

"How close were they?"

"Very."

Frank looked directly at Louis. "So close, in fact, that my acquaintances dummied up a body, filled in phony dental records, placed some fake fingerprints on the car, and set it on fire. And Louis, my dear brother, you are dead, dead, dead."

The thunder filled the room, the lightening crackled and the lights flickered.

"Jesus Christ, Frank – what the fuck – I thought you said no one knew me, what I was ; now I come home and you tell me I am dead?"

"Easy, easy, Lou. As I said, people were getting too close and we couldn't have them coming up and directly accusing you. So before that happened – you died. Case closed. Everyone wanted a – pardon the expression – Happy Ending, and they got it. Close the damn case and lose it. Gone, finito, The End.

Louis half rose. "Frank, I'm dead. What do I do, what do I do? I'm back, but how do I live?"

"I'm glad you asked. Sit down and I'll explain."

Louis sat and wondered, "what is my brother up to?"

"Here it is in a nutshell. You are an intelligent, relatively young –"

"Yeah right."

"Hey let me finish – anyway as I said. The group I am associated with watched you closely 34 years ago – and also have watched you and kept you safe, during your, shall we say, extended vacation down South."

"You what? Watched, kept me safe, what the fuck are you talking about? All those years you babysat me?"

"How do you think you lived and who did you think found you the job that paid so well with no ID except your word?"

"Hey – I made that job and improved myself and worked my way up."

"Yes, you did. As I said before, you're smart, a go getter and many other things that my group –"

"What group? What the hell are you talking about?" Louis said, becoming more agitated. "What the hell is going on?"

"As I said, you fit all the qualifications we need for the job; let's use that terminology for what we want you to do."

"What do you mean? What in the world are you talking about --"

"Look, Lou, in a few minutes you will meet a man – a man who will explain further what I have alluded to, and then you can make a decision which I am sure will benefit you greatly."

The rain was still coming down in torrents and through a slight opening in the door you could hear the wind howling – trying to get in but not succeeding.

"Well Frank, I'll listen to the man because that seems to be an option and from the way things are looking I have very few of those."

"Look Louis, it's not like you had a lot of options when you left. You did some pretty bad things – one doesn't go around killing and becomes President."

"Right."

As if on cue, the bell rang.

"He's here, I'll get it."

"Fine – no problem. I'm your captive audience."

Some murmuring could be heard. A man, slightly stooped with a tan raincoat down to the ankles and belted at the waist, walked in.

He had on granny glasses which he was wiping with a handkerchief. Frank took his coat and introduced Louis to Malcolm Fletcher. Fletcher shrugged out of the coat and nodded.

"Hello Louis, I'm glad to see you arrived alright and seem to be in good health, from all reports." He spoke with a slight accent.

"Well, Mr. Fletcher, I don't know if I'm glad to see you."

"Louis!!!"

"It's alright, Frank," Fletcher held up his hand – "I understand."

"Well, you're a group of one or maybe two, if you count Frank. What the hell is going on?"

"Quite right, quite right. Let's all sit down and I'll go over what is going to happen –"

"What might happen –"

Fletcher looked at Louis with a steel glint in his eye. "Sit down and I'll talk ... you listen."

Both men sat. Frank went to get drinks.

"Here's your amaretto, Malcolm. Your water, Louis. Okay guys, let's talk."

CHAPTER FIFTEEN

"Alright Louis, did Frank say anything to you about your past history?"

"Yeah, he said I'm dead, that you guys evidently had my back down South and that there is something here you want me to do."

"Correct. You are dead, in fact we went so far as to put a cross on 75 where the car burned, and every few months put flowers there – at first. Now it's just a cross. Empty, but there."

"Back then you killed a lot of people for a reason you felt was justified. Personally, I think you were a little crazy . . ."

"I was a lot crazy. I was hurting in a great depression over the only woman who loved me as I was ... who trusted me ... my whole being was with her, and then she died. My fault, society's fault – people's fault. I hated them. I got back at them ... the one way I knew would hurt them."

"Yes, you did. And for a man with limited resources and equipment, you did a remarkable job. That is what brought you to our attention. Anybody can shoot someone, but not everyone, my boy, can pull it off with such panache."

"Thanks, I guess." Louis crossed his leg and looked at Fletcher. "But in the past years I have lived with it and passed it on – it's the past and gone. I went over and over killing those people. Taking that one thing that makes them unique, that makes them an Alice or Frank. Their life. I have lived with that for 34 years and finally moved on."

"To you, not to those that you killed or their families. They still remember and mourn and hate. That's why we killed you."

"That's nice, but . . .?"

"Louis," Frank broke in, "if you hadn't left when you did, we were going to kill you."

"What?"

"Don't be surprised." Frank went on, "You did a lot of damage. In fact, the reason we let you go on was that some of that damage worked in our favor and achieved some goals we had in mind –"

"That's why when you escaped, I covered you, gave you the money and the route out – and kept you happy and safe all these years. "

"We want you to work for us; we want you to do some things for us legally, and with all the power of the United States Government behind it."

"What the fuck are you talking about?" Louis got up, walked around the chair and sat down. "I'm going to be what – a spy? A secret agent? You're all nuts," his hand shaking as he picked up his glass.

CHAPTER SIXTEEN

"Look, Louis. I feel, we feel," gesturing towards Frank, "we all feel what you did was misguided and killed people unnecessarily, but as far as a military operation goes – fantastic."

"You mean like 9/11?"

"Yes, horrible though it was – militarily, it was as fine an operation as has been carried out."

"To take those people and practically bring a nation to its knees was brilliant. At the same time we do not condone it, or even applaud it. War is never good to anyone."

"Anyway, moving along. You Louis, are a one man army, and fit into our plans perfectly. You are like an uncut diamond, very rough, but we can train you, hone you, smooth you out . . ."

Frank broke in, "Until you are the perfect weapon for the job. You and a group of highly trained people can perform the operation we have in mind. America is in dangerous times, and will only continue to exist as long as we surpass our enemies and beat them at every turn."

"So, it's going to be very tough." He took a sip of water, his mouth dry. "My life is going to be like a person in witness protection, a new life, name, cover . . ."

"Exactly, Louis, that is what is going to happen to you. Your cover will probably be that of a traveling representative, so that will account for your not being at home all the time. To train you, we will send you to our "factory". Anonymity is the password. We only attack those items which are truly dangerous. We go to our enemies' level. Too long we have said we will not stoop to our enemies' level. They expect us to not go down to that level. But to succeed, we must."

"What if I say no, what happens? I disappear, go away?"

"No, no my dear Louis – we will give you your new identification and you will become a "normal" person. If you do accept our offer, you will do so knowing you'll be doing good for your country and most importantly taking out bad guys legally and live a very fulfilling life.

"Hey – I know what I did, I have come to grips with it during the past 34 years, Alice knows what I did and she forgives me."

"Does she really, Louis? We have watched you these past years, listened to you, heard your nightmares of Alice not approving of what you did."

"You bugged my house? Why . . ."

Louis, we watched and listened because if things worked out, we wanted you. So let's cut the bullshit Louis, you are going to work for us. You're going to find you like it." He patted Louis on the shoulder.

"So dear boy, let's avoid the histrionics and get ready to move."

Louis looked at Fletcher and Frank, sat back in the chair, closed his eyes and could see Alice with the ghosts in his mind. She smiled and nodded her head. He sat up.

"Okay boys, I'm yours. Let's get this dog and pony show on the road."

CHAPTER SEVENTEEN

Two months have passed. Louis, now newly named Christopher Thomas Wolf, has been relocated into a small Connecticut town in a mostly rural setting. It has a main street with a few streets shooting out of the main one. A town square with a pond in the middle of it, which in winter serves as a skating rink ringed by fir trees, and a church with a pointed steeple off to the side. Wolf lived outside of a town in a blue split level Colonial house. Topped off with blue shutters, a fireplace, and a two car garage. His cover job was that of a manufacturing representative of farm and road construction equipment, of which he had zero knowledge of. But through mail order courses and a couple of weeks of classes with an actual manufacturing company and hands on training, he had become familiar with his product, and through that made his cover more believable. He also made several acquaintances in the business.

Although he had just finished his second week at his new house, he had completed a couple of recons of the area of and near his home. He also had installed some light sensors and miniature cameras.

The doorbell chimed.

"Coming, coming!" as he went to the door. He opened it and found himself looking into the eyes of a slightly Rubenesque, 45-50 year old woman with light brown hair and slightly pink lipstick on her full mouth and a glimmer in her eyes.

"Hello there, my name is Barbra. Barbra Dean. I came with this apple pie to welcome you to the neighborhood."

"Come in, come in. I looked around and saw a house about a mile and a half down the road. I take it that's yours?"

"You got it. It's comfortable, good location and paid for." She walked in and brushed by him with sweat running along his chest.

"Here, let me take that. I'll put it in the kitchen. Do you want some now?"

"Sure, if it's no trouble, a small piece and maybe some coffee. I passed by your house and when the for sale sign came down, and the sold one went up, I made a mental note to stop by. Plus I was curious."

Wolf put down the pie on the coffee table. "Well," he thought, "Not bad looking, definitely candid and sort of explains how she knew when I moved in."

He put on the coffee and walked back into the living room.

"Sit, sit, relax." Barbra moved to the chair facing the couch and sat down.

"Thank you. Well, I finally get to see who moved in. You know I'm Barb. What's your name?"

"Christopher Thomas Wolf. I'm a sales rep for farm and road equipment. I travel around quite a bit and right now, I am on a small vacation with pay until someone decides they want to buy. I also have a couple of schools to go to that will help keep me abreast of anything new that is coming out in the field, and of course I get paid for attending."

"Sounds good to me, luckily I have a job as an administrator at St. Joseph's Hospital. The pay is good and I have a health plan and a small pension, so I consider myself very lucky."

Wolf had gone back into the kitchen. "How do you like your coffee?"

"A little milk and two sugars, please." He made the coffee and came back in, "Here you go," placing it on the coffee table in front of her.

"Thank you, kind sir."

"Anything for a pretty lady."

Wolf and Barb continued to talk for a couple of hours, finding they agreed more than disagreed. He liked baseball (the Yankees) and football (Giants) and she liked hockey (New York Rangers). Wolf heard the bangs of his grandfather clock.

"My God has it really been three hours since you got here? Where has the time gone?"

"See, that's what happens when you meet someone you like – time just flies."

"I know, I was married before."

"Oh? I didn't realize."

"Yes, it was a long time ago. We were young – everything was good, then I lost my job and things just fell apart."

Wolf got a little angry – society was to blame. Not enough jobs. People didn't care. The middle class got much smaller but the responsibility bigger.

"She got sick – died."

"Oh, I am so sorry. I've been lucky – no one's died and I never had a husband, just lived my own life and enjoyed it."

"I felt so lonely and without guidance. Just out there. But I found something to do."

"That's good. I understand you should find something to do to pass the time, keep yourself busy."

Wolf smiled a half smile, "Well, you could say I kept busy for a while, then I took a long vacation. I miss her, but I finally accepted she was gone."

"Anyway, time has gone by, I'm hungry. What about dinner? I know we just met, but what the hell?"

"I agree – what if I go home, shower, get ready and then you come and get me and we go out?"

"Sound good to me. How about I pick you up in about two hours?"

"Fine, I'll see you then. Do you need directions?"

"No, I know where you are –"

Barb got up, brought the cups and plates to the kitchen, put them in the sink.

"I'll get that – you just go and make yourself beautiful. Or should I say, enhance the beauty you already have." Barb came by, touched his face lightly, kissed his cheek lightly and said goodbye. He went to the window and watched her drive away.

He liked her, but what would this lead to? His work came first – he was committed – he signed. He spoke to himself, "well, let's just see what happens. Live today and let tomorrow take care of itself."

CHAPTER EIGHTEEN

He was dressed in a blue blazer, open neck blue shirt and tan pants with black patent shoes. She came to the door in a nice black cocktail dress, slight décolletage with high heels and looked very good.

"You look lovely," he held the door for her as she walked by, brushing close to him. "Thank you – it's just something I put together in an hour or so. The things we do to make ourselves attractive for you men."

"Well," looking her up and down slowly and opening the car door, "I'll tell you, I find it very enjoyable. You look almost edible I mean . . ."

"I know what you mean – take it easy and as far as edible, we'll see later."

He blushed and she could see it if it wasn't night.

"How about we go to the Longhorn? It just opened up and has excellent steaks, and if you're not interested in steak, it has a varied menu. Suitable to your culinary taste," he bowed.

"Sounds good to me. Let's go."

They arrived in a little over half an hour.

"Yes sir, we can fix you up with a table. Come this way, please."

Wolf looked around and spotted a table in the corner. "I'd like that table over there, if you don't mind."

"Of course sir, it's available."

As Wolf approached the table he pulled out the chair for Barbra and took the chair across from her, which put his back to the wall. He had a clear view of the entire room, along with the entrance.

"Joanna will be your waitress. Before she comes, would you like anything to drink?"

"Whiskey and ginger ale for me on the rocks. Barb, would you like anything?"

"Yes, thank you. I'd like scotch on the rocks."

"Very good, I'll have that for you in a moment – meanwhile, here are some menus. Joanna will be here in a few minutes."

Wolf looked over the room and then at Barb. "Well, Barb, how do you like it so far?"

"It's very nice – the bulls head and western paraphernalia definitely give credence to its name."

"So ... how did you pick St. Joe's to work at?"

"It's a small but very good hospital. Not like other hospitals where colic in a baby is a very big deal. I wouldn't go to any one of those. So how did you get into the construction equipment field?"

"Well, it is a huge field with new products coming along almost every day. People have to eat and build, so hence farm and construction. Also I have a bit of wanderlust in me and being single, I can go practically anywhere at any given time. But as I said things are slow due to the economy, but I've got my name in for several schools with pay – which will tide me over. So it isn't a bad deal."

Dinner came and went – they talked and enjoyed themselves.

"Well, it's getting late," Barb said, "And I have to go to work tomorrow."

"Of course, of course. Joanna, could we have the check. Thank you."

"Well, I really enjoyed tonight. By the way, what do they call you, Chris or Wolf or what?"

"I answer to both, to my friends Chris, to my enemies Wolf. I find sometimes it's more intimidating and in my business you need every edge you can get."

"Well Chris, about coming in for some coffee?..."

"Sure. I'd like that." They walked into the house. He noticed she had colonial furniture. Well, colonial scenes on the fabric. One large couch – one easy chair – and a rocker. Dark pine wood. Couple of lantern like lamps and two prints of Early American by Wysocki, and a fireplace.

"Nice place, very cozy."

"Have a seat, I'll do the coffee and bring it in here. You can start a fire. All the stuff is right there."

"Right, I see it – first put on an artificial log and light it?"

"Yup, that's all."

Coffee fragrance wafted through to the living room.

"How do you like your coffee?"

"Just black – it's sort of an acquired taste – I learned to drink it that way. Because if there's no sugar or milk the taste isn't the same but if you like black, everything is fine."

"Okay," she said as she came into the room with the coffee. "You're easy to please."

They looked at the fire, heard the crackle as the flames turned orange and red.

Wolf turned toward Barbra and kissed her – it was a long slow kiss tongues fitting against each other, little bites on the lips and slow kisses on the side of the neck. Breathing becomes more intense feeling each other with soft touches. She rubbing him, he running his hand, along her thigh – moans of pleasure coming from both of them.

CHAPTER NINETEEN

Wolf put down the phone. Rubbed his eyes. "Awake cruel world," and got out of bed. Passing his clock "3:30, what the hell? I've heard of the early bird catching the worm, but this could lead to total annihilation of all wormdom," he gave his half-smile.

He slept in the nude, a habit he had picked up with Alice and they saw no reason to change it. She always wore a nightgown and said it is sexier to take off but she liked him with no clothes. He still missed her.

He went into the bathroom, looked into the mirror saw a mature man, with a Peter Pan attitude looking back at him. Dark brown hair with flecks of gray that when he was out in the sun too long showed reddish highlights. Piercing dark brown eyes; which when he was in high school looked at Mr. Castagno with such anger – the teacher had yelled at him not to look at him that way. His grandfather had a stare like that.

"Oh well, life's a bitch."

He finished in the bathroom, went back into the bedroom, arranged his clothes and items and started to dress.

He selected an L.L. Bean blue travel shirt of which he had several. They wore well, had Velcro flap pockets, which made it easy to take items out of, and dried quickly.

He finished dressing, took out his Fischer space pen, nitrogen filled which could write in any position, write on any surface and was a great stabbing weapon. He also had a small waterproof note pad, good for notes and also a great weapon to slice a throat or cut across eyes. He put these in a shirt pocket. A handkerchief rolled with a switchblade also made a good bandage, woven belt a sling or tourniquet.

He put on his safari jacket with Velcro flaps and the .45 caliber Derringer went into the lower right hand pocket. He was dressed, he felt at ease. He was grabbing his leather carpenter style bag when a loud knock sounded at the door. The knock sounded again – he walked warily but silently to the door. Took out his gun, stood to the side and quickly opened the door. He pushed his gun out and into the person's chest very quickly. He had hit the man in the lower chest with the barrel of his weapon.

"What do you want?" he snarled. "Who the hell are you?" He questioned, pushing the neck back a little more.

The man nearly 6 feet tall, slim, wearing a Nomex flight suit smiled, put up his hands, and said "My mother told me there'd be days like this." I'm sorry to have made you nervous, Mr. Wolf, I should have been quieter. My name is Major Joe Biernacki and I'm your guide to Alpha." He put out his hand.

CHAPTER TWENTY

Wolf put down his gun and place it back into his pocket.

"Okay major. In my business, you can't avoid being too careful."

"You got it, Mr. Wolf. I totally understand the situation. I'll take your bag. I'm glad it's only one. That's all you'll need here. By the way, call me Joe."

"Okay Joe, and to my friends I'm Chris. Let me lock up and we'll go."

The door locked, Wolf followed Joe to his ride. A huge black helicopter smelling of parts warming and oil. He knew it was a dangerous weapon..

"Here we go, Chris." Joe opened the door like hatch, pulled down a two step ladder, shoved Wolf's bag in.

Wolf got in, Joe closed the door, walked to the other side of the chopper and got in.

"By the way," Joe called, "This in Capt. Richard LaCoste – the best darn pilot, other than me, you could come across."

The interior lights were dim, but Chris could make out LaCoste's sort of round face with a smile on it.

"Don't believe everything you hear Mr. Wolf – only all of the good stuff. The bad stuff is either bullshit or envy."

"Okay, Captain?"

"Call me Rich or Dick."

"I've been down this road before. Dick, Call me Chris or Wolf."

"Okay Wolf, I like that it's so, so, dramatic." LaCoste laughed.

Wolf smiled, "Alright guys, I see we get along just fine but it doesn't mean we'll get married soon."

Biernacki grinned and turned, "Right, by your right side is a helmet, it'll be yours. It will fit you and also it makes it easier to communicate with us."

"Okay – found it."

Joe and Dick talked to each other, flipped on switches. Lights came on, a whirl could be heard and before Wolf realized it, they went straight up 3,000-4,000 feet with no sound.

"Where's all the noise, how do we move so fast? What is this?"

Dick announced, "You are now in an S-76B Eagle gunship. Two rotary 50 caliber cannons and enough missiles to bring down a small town."

"We have a small nuclear turbine with silenced stealth mode in an engine and rotary system, that's why when we came down you couldn't hear us. We can land right next to you and all you'd heard is a small whisper with our modified blades. With the stealth chip, it knocks out any radar laser beams from seeing us."

"Also Chris," broke in Joe, "we have what is called in the business an ITT IRCM. It's an infrared counter measure."

"Meaning what?" Wolf asked, as he looked out the window and saw the earth flying by.

"Meaning," said Biernacki , "That when a missile launches on us – if it's ground to air, it's less than two miles away. Making its flight time less than 5 seconds before contact. Our little baby here takes less than 2 seconds to react. It has nothing to do with the crew, it works independently. It tracks the missile and blinds it with a laser shot from the undercarriage of the ship. It's attached to a fiber optic box placed in the hell hole. The Navy has its J Task, we have this borrowed from the Army."

"ITT – makes the fiber optics and IRCM the rest. Started in 2004, came out 2008. Nice little baby, and all ours."

"I am impressed. Guys, I'm going to get a little shut eye – I'm tired."

"No problem, Wolf. Just relax and we'll let you know when we get there in a couple of hours."

Wolf closed his eyes, the lights went dim. He thought of Alice and a lump came to his throat. He thought of Barbra and he got a little excited. "That's the way of the world." he smiled. "Up and down." He fell asleep.

CHAPTER TWENTY-ONE

The subtle thump, thump of the rotor blade broke through Wolf's sleep. Rubbing his eyes, he was refreshed, secure in this impregnable, man-made womb. He felt there was very little, if anything, that could harm him.

He sat up, looked around. Through the side window the sun was everywhere casting a bright light into the cabin.

Major Biernacki was watching a screen on the consul in front of him, which showed the rear compartment, noticed Wolf was awake, "Hey stranger, welcome back to the living. You were sleeping like the dead."

"Yes I was and I thoroughly enjoyed every minute of it."

"I know what you mean, way up here with all this electronics and fire power – you feel invincible," exclaimed LaCoste.

"If you want Wolf, there's a seat up here on the right that will give you a look at your new home."

Wolf came forward, "That's it," said Biernacki, "Just pull it up, secure it by that leg and you can sit forward and see, Alpha."

CHAPTER TWENTY-TWO

The sight that met Wolf's eyes was unforgettable. It would be like hearing the National Anthem over and over again and not getting tired of it.

Out there over a desert plain, not so very far away was a silver spot growing bigger and bigger with each passing second. It quickly filled the whole front window of the aircraft. It was, to put it simply, a mountain, a big huge primeval piece of rock towering over all.

It was silver in color – no hold on – it was black, yes, a huge black plateau raising high into the sky.

It reminded him of a jungle cat or a wolf waiting for its prey, waiting to pounce. The silver was in the rock and looked like a beast showing its fangs.

"Hold on, here we go," shouted Biernacki, breaking into Wolf's thoughts. He winked at LaCoste."You know Major, you're breaking protocol and Control is not going to like this one little, little bit. They're going to be very pissed at us."

"Yeah, you're right, but what the hell – you only live once."

"Maj, that's a very trite saying to get us into this. It's true but, oh hell, let's do it. Our court martial will be glorious."

"Oh stop complaining – look at it this way. We'll give Mr. Wolf a ride he'll never forget."

"Hold on Wolf," exclaimed Biernacki, "Here we go!" He pulled back on the stick and the bird leaped up, pushing you back into the seat. Faster and faster – up, up in a rapid climb. The chopper was so close to the side of the mountain that points of rock whizzing by looked touchable. It was like one of those rides at Disney where you went sooo fast – only this one was going up.

Suddenly a moment of silence erupted as the bird flew over the crest of the mountain. Ahead of Wolf in the morning sunlight was Alpha, raising high into the sky. A huge mirror like crystalline structure, beckoning you forward, forward.

CHAPTER TWENTY-THREE

"This is Control to Major Biernacki. You are cleared for landing on Pad 3." They could sense the disapproval in Control's voice.

"Roger Control, we have Mr. Wolf on board, over."

"Good, we assume he is in one piece (definitely disapproval) – let Captain LaCoste take care of the chopper and you bring Mr. Wolf over to see Crafton for his briefing."

"Good to go, Control, will do. Out."

They brought the chopper in on Pad 3, "Nice and soft Major, just like a baby's butt," said LaCoste as the bird landed.

"No problem – with once again the two best pilots in Alpha handling the controls. I'll tie down, while you take Wolf over to Crafton."

They climbed down from the chopper. Wolf grabbed his bag and walked over to Biernacki, who pointed him to a vehicle that resembled a golf cart with sides and a roof. He threw his bag in the rear, got in as Biernacki pushed the ignition, and off they went.

"I've got a question. I thought Fletcher ran this – who's Grafton?"

"He does run this place – but Grafton is like the welcome wagon to newbies. He gives them some idea as to how the place is run, what will be expected of you, show you to your room, where if memory serves me correctly, will be all the clothes you will need for your training here."

"They know my size?"

Biernacki smiled. "They know everything."

CHAPTER TWENTY-FOUR

Biernacki drove Wolf over to the front of the building which was more intimidating the closer they got. It rose up into the powder blue sky without a flaw, seamless in its integrity.

Biernacki turned to Wolf, "I'll leave you off now and meet you around 1700 hours for dinner."

"Fine, I'll meet you then and – oh, thanks for the ride. It was indescribable."

Biernacki smiled, waved. Wolf grabbed his bag and walked to the entrance.

"It's like any other big beautiful building," he smiled. The door slid open. As he proceeded forward he noticed an array of potted plants, chairs and sofas, all arranged so that the front desk was the main focal point. You were gently but subtly moved, moved forward to that desk. The lighting was low but bright, the walls were colored in tans and blues with music softly playing. In this case, it was "Ol' Man River" from Showboat – "just keep trudgin' along." He wondered if it was a hint of what was to come.

A man, a fairly rotund man, greeted him. He had a scar running across his face from the right eye, which was gone, across his nose, down to his chin. He was well groomed, neat and clean. His hands were thick and big. He smiled – which it was not.

"Ah Mr. Christopher Wolf, welcome, so pleased to meet you," he extended his right hand and Wolf's hand was engulfed in it. "Do come over and sign in." He placed a pen on the desk and turned around a sign in sheet. "Just there, very good, thank you."

He took the sheet, placed it in a drawer. Pinned to the man's suit breast pocket was a name tag – white enamel with a gold A, a name in black letters under it. Jules Grafton, FFL.

Wolf nodded, "Hello, Mr. Grafton. How're you? I've heard so many good things about you."

"I see, probably from my esteemed compatriots, Biernacki and LaCoste. Good pilots, but sometimes crazier than bed bugs."

"I believe they gave you the grand tour – up?"

Wolf smiled. "Ah, they did. I could say I found it quite uplifting, but I won't."

"I like you already, Jules, for your great insight. So what's in store for me now?"

Jules reached into the drawer, pulled out some paperwork, handed it to Wolf. "I'll take you up to your room, where you can fill the forms out. Now if you'll follow me, I'll take you there."

He came around the desk, grabbed Wolf's bag, and went to a tank of elevators. Wolf noticed he walked with a slight limp in his left leg.

He noticed the emblems on the door. "I take it everything is emblazoned with that sign."

"Yes, it is to give civilians coming in the semblance of a corporate headquarters with officers upstairs."

He turned toward Wolf – pulled a card from his pocket. "You're in Suite 1515, the view will be nice."

"Thank you Jules, I appreciate the heads up."

They stepped into the elevator, the feeling of speed was imperceptible, but they reached the 15th floor in a matter of seconds. A chime signaled the opening of the doors.

"To your right, Mr. Wolf. It's the second door on your left."

"Thank you, and please call me Christopher or Wolf."

"Very well, thank you Wolf." and he bowed a little, putting his arm out indicating they had reached Wolf's room. "'*Nous sommes arrives*,' we have arrived, Wolf. Welcome to Alpha."

Wolf opened the door. It was a very good welcome indeed, as he stepped over the threshold and looked around.

CHAPTER TWENTY-FIVE

Wolf walked into the room. It resembled a small cabin, then a hotel room. Jules broke into his thoughts, "This is the great room, the chairs and couch are comfortable, the gas light fireplace works, and the windows offer a panoramic view. On a clear day, you can see twenty miles out."

He moved to the left. "The kitchen is small, but has all the necessary appliances in case you don't want to go to the dining room. In back, as you can see, is a small eating area." He walked down a small hallway, "Here is your den, your study area as it were. Everything here – the books, DVDs, etc. are all necessary for the training you will take."

He walked out, down the hall about 10 feet, opened a door. "Here's your bedroom, with adjoining bath. The bathroom has a whirlpool which from time to time you will find necessary to use. Once again, the view is excellent. You are expected to clean up after yourself. If you are indisposed – say, an accident from training – we have a cleaning staff on duty 24-7 to assist you. Also the same for medical."

"After all this, that last little piece of news makes me so sure I'm in the right hands."

"Yes, quite – we are here to serve." He walked over to a double door. "Here is your closet; in here are your everyday clothes and training clothes. Weapons, packs, etc. will be issued to you as needed for that period of training."

"Once again Jules, I'm impressed as to the effort you – or should I say Alpha – has gone to to make me comfortable, and – it sounds like – everyone else."

"Not at all, '*mon ami*, that's it exactly. Our people, we are a team, whether it is an individual effort or a group effort, we are here to help and aid you in whatever way possible, day or night. We keep you well and you do your job. We work with one another. Now, I'll leave you to the small amount of paperwork you have – dinner is at 1700 hours in the dining hall. Dress is casual – any questions before I depart?"

"I have plenty, but I'll hold off, however there is one question – I notice on your name tag it has FFL, what's it mean?"

"Ah, my astute friend, that is where I served before I became employed at Alpha. It gives our new people an idea of where the staff originated and the expertise they are faced with, and to the civilians the guise of, pardon me – the act of hiring a vet, non-discriminatory and all that."

"Anyhow, to your question, the FFL stands for the French Foreign Legion. The eye comes from a scrimmage with some disgruntled Arabs and the limp from Alpha. The beauty of all this, is if you are, shall we say, somewhat disabled in an Alpha project and wish to continue aboard with Alpha you may. They will find you a position suitable to your, how shall I say, your problem. Other than that you are eligible for retirement."

"By retire – I take it to mean, a nice little house, health benefits and all that."

"Why Mr. Wolf," Jules gave a slight bow and walked to the door, "What other kind of retirement is there?"

The door closed softly.

"Right."

CHAPTER TWENTY-SIX

When Jules had left, Wolf took the paperwork over to the desk.

"Well let's look and see what Santa has left." The documents were few and consisted of a will, health insurance packet and, yes it was, a retirement package with options to be checked.

"Well I'll be damned," he exclaimed. "Son of a bitch. Looks like maybe I will have retirement in my future, but I haven't even started yet. Let's see what happens. Time for dinner, I'll go meet Biernacki and see what's up."

He took the elevator up to the sixty-first floor, got out, went right. The room was set up in a circular fashion with booths set at the outer edge and then separate tables and chairs set in the inner area. The aroma of foods hit his nostrils – he inhaled and was filled with hunger.

"Smells good, huh?" Biernacki said.

"It surely does, didn't realize how hungry I was."

"Well, let's go get some – LaCoste is holding down a table."

The food was displayed – some in cases, some in buffet style, from steaks, to chops, to fish, to an array of vegetables and fruits.

"The food is excellent, the choice is immense. They treat you well here, because out in the field, things can get pretty dicey."

"You didn't have to tell me that Joe I remember what you had, or rather didn't have, on the field. That shit stays with you. Anyway, let's eat."

They both grabbed some steaks and potatoes and headed over to a booth. Passing several tables with people eating – Joe acknowledges several people and greeted others warmly, introducing Wolf to all of them.

"Depending on what you need in the field, you will probably work with most of the people in this room at one time or another. They all have their own field of experience and have quite a bit of knowledge in other areas as well, as you will have after your training. Here, sit down –"

Wolf smiled. "Richard – how're you doing?"

"Fine, Mr. Wolf – grabbed some food just before you arrived. How'd you like your room?"

"What's not to like when your room is set up like a small palace? Jules was very helpful. So," looking at both men, "what happens now?"

"Tomorrow you get an in-briefing that tells you a little of Alpha and its workings, then you get a psych eval, then the next day your training starts."

"Most of it is perfunctory," chimed in LaCoste, "If you're here, you're already in. Tomorrow is the period of turning the screen so as to make you realize you're in."

"Sounds like fun. It'll be interesting to find out why I'm in, other than the fact I had no other options."

"Oh, you had options, Mr. Wolf," replied LaCoste. "Some of them you would probably not like."

"Do tell, Rich, do tell."

CHAPTER TWENTY-SEVEN

Wolf woke up. He saw a message had been left on his phone.

"Good morning Mr. Wolf, my name is Dr. Sinclair, and if possible I would like to meet with you at 1000 hours. My office 4407 is across the walkway in Building Two. Have a good day, and I'll see you at 10."

Wolf put down the phone, walking to his desk, retrieved the building directory, found Building Two and Sinclair's office. It was a shot way from his room so he decided to eat. Went to the fridge, took out some bread and butter and strawberry jam. Made toast, coffee, and got dressed. He went down the hall to the elevator, went to the 44th floor and followed the signs to Building Two. A sign pointed around a corner. As Wolf turned the corner he came to an abrupt halt. There in front of him was Building Two, but to reach it you had to walk through a clear acrylic tube of about 100 feet. As he stepped into the tube, a bird soared past beneath his feet. He looked down and whistled, "Man, to see the doctor here, you must really be sick." He also noticed a red arrow on the wall, pointing to a box of glasses that according to the instructions would turn the tube dark for those that didn't like heights.

He moved through the tube to Building Two. Dr. Sinclair's office was the 3rd door on the right. He knew from the directory that most doctors' offices were here. The entrance was a large white door with the typical gold "A". He opened the door which gave off a small chime and stepped in. The light was bright but at the same time quiet and blended in with the green and tan of the place. Several chairs, sofas and tables were placed around. At a desk off to the side was sitting a lovely brunette typing away. She looked up. Smiled.

"Mr. Christopher Wolf?"

"None other."

"Dr. Sinclair is expecting you. Have a seat and I'll let him know you're here."

"Thank you," Wolf sat.

Miss Jenkins pushed a button on her head phone.

"Dr. Sinclair, Mr. Wolf has arrived."

"Yes, I'll send him in."

"Go right in Mr. Wolf, right through that door."

"Thank you – uh – Miss Jenkins is it?"

"Yes, Belinda Jenkins, most people call me Linda."

Wolf smiled and raised an eyebrow.

"Well Linda, since I'm most people, I'll call you that also and you can call me Chris."

She gave a delightful little laugh, "Just go right in, Chris. See you soon."

He looked at her again, looked at her name badge. Under her name was the acronym FBI.

"As soon as I get out."

CHAPTER TWENTY-EIGHT

"Come in, come in, Mr. Wolf. It's a pleasure to finally meet you. Your file is very, very thick and quite impressive."

Wolf sat down in a chair in front of Sinclair's desk.

"So you're the shrink – what for – pardon my bluntness – do you read my mind and tell me what kind of nut case I am and how that qualifies me for this job?"

"No, no. Nothing so dramatic as in the movies. Through all those years of watching you, we know your capabilities and are duly impressed."

Sinclair, a small man in a white linen, sleeve folded up shirt. His tie loose. He had a round face, a little bald on top and wore small gold-rimmed glasses. He sat back, pointed his fingers together and forced them into a tent like figure.

"No, no, Mr. Wolf," he adjusted his glasses, "You would never had heard of Alpha if you had not passed our requirements, and as you so quaintly put it, are definitely not a nut case. As I stated before, having watched you during your resting and shall we say, growing up period down South, you are in remarkably good health and sound of mind."

"So what am I here for, Doc? If I passed, why the talk? I'm sure you're a busy man in this place."

"That's exactly why you're here, just to talk. A friendly little get together to let you know I'm here for you at any time. Day or night, we will be here for you. As far as this job goes," he looked directly at Wolf, "Your reason for being and staying here is retribution to make up for the wrongs you've done, and you're going to try to do good, that's why you'll stay."

"So it's that simple? No elaborate studies, no probings, nothing?"

"If you were a regular agent coming into the fold – yes – there'd be tests and probes, as you put it, but since you are not, because we know you so well – none of that is necessary. Just a touching of base so to speak. To let you know we are here for you, at any time."

"That's it?"

"That's it, Mr. Wolf. You are free to go back to your suite."

Wolf got up, walked to the door.

"Thanks Doc, knowing you're here helps and if I need you, all I have to do is whistle."

The doctor rose from the desk and smiled, "If you need me, Mr. Wolf, you'll do more than whistle!"

CHAPTER TWENTY-NINE

Wolf walked slowly back to his room. "Well, they certainly want you to have a mind set that they're here 24/7, of course it also means they're watching you 24/7. Considering the situation and what goes on here, which I'm wondering about, I can see why the precautions and the nicely worded phrases of being here.

I guess retribution is as good a reason as any to work here. God, country, and conscience does make heroes of us all." He walked gingerly through the tube and opened his door.

He saw his phone was flashing again.

"This place is busier than Grand Central Station."

He pushed a button.

"Mr. Wolf, this is Professor Joseph Alcorn speaking. I will be your official welcoming committee to Alpha.

Tomorrow morning at 0915 hours a meeting will take place in the small auditorium and will be a get together of you and specially selected others for an overview of Alpha. You need not eat breakfast as a small breakfast buffet will be set up for all. Dress is casual. Please be prompt. I so detest waiting for the last person to show. IT's so impolite and in some cultures disastrous. Thank you and see you tomorrow morning. I did say on time, didn't I?"

CHAPTER THIRTY

Wolf woke up early. He was filled with anticipation as a little boy on his birthday, excited for the day ahead, to get to those presents and see what's there.

He ate a strawberry-banana yogurt to still his stomach, did some exercises, dressed and left.

He arrived ten minutes early, remembering the message Alcorn had left. He walked into the auditorium and saw that others had arrived and were talking.

The auditorium had stadium seating, but enough room up front to put in a circular table, chairs, and two long rectangular tables end to end. The two tables no doubt for the buffet, and the other table for who? Arthur and his knights. He smiled at the image.

The walls in front and to the sides were opaque with wallpaper like finish that gave off a slight glow. The American flag was to the right facing out, and the Alpha flag to his left.

A slim balding man in a tweed suit with vest, maroon bow tie and blue shirt was at the side talking with Biernacki and LaCoste.

He wondered why they were there. He walked down to them. He looked at the people and smiled. They smiled back.

"Hello Joe, Rich. How're you doing? Didn't expect to see you here." LaCoste waved, with a slight movement of his hand.

"Fine Wolf, Rich and I are getting along famously and as to the why and wherefore, this handsome looking gentleman will explain all.

Professor Joseph Alcorn, may I present Christopher Wolf. Chris, this is Professor Alcorn."

Both men looked at each other and shook hands. On Professor Alcorn's badge was HRT. The Professor noticed his glance and gave a smile.

"It's for Hostage Release Team. Alpha felt with my special skills, I was the right person to introduce new people to each other, and to Alpha and Natalie."

His glance encompassed the others in the room. He looked at his watch and clapped his hands – the room grew brighter and the soft music faded and stopped. The people looked up.

"All right, everyone, if I could have your attention. You'll notice the table in front of you."

"It's hard not to notice," spoke up the woman with silver hair.

The Professor laughed, "Yes it is, isn't it. Anyway, on the table are cards with each of your names. Please find your place and have a seat. I see by the head count you are all here and on time. With that, I am pleased and because of that no one will lose theirs."

CHAPTER THIRTY-ONE

"Good morning everyone. I'm so glad you all could make it. I know all of you are familiar with Major Biernacki and Captain LaCoste," he nodded to them, seated one on each side of him. Both men nodded to the group.

"They brought all of you here to Alpha and for all intents and purposes will be attached to your team during training and for actual missions. In order to work and perform at your best, you have to know your people and trust them. As both men flew you here, you have the start of a rapport with them and they with you.

Now, Monsieurs Biernacki and LaCoste will hand out two Velcro name tags to each of you, one for your uniform, and the other for your casual clothes."

Biernacki walked over to the woman and handed her the badges. "Wear them in good health," he smiled.

She smiled, "Thanks, Major, I will."

Susie Havel was about five feet five inches tall, about 130 pounds. Her hair was white (premature) with a dark tan.

Weapons were her specialty on the team, and if the occasion called for a woman, she was it. Her dad wanted her to know all about weapons as he was an avid hunter.

LaCoste walked over to a six foot six giant. Bald, which was self-inflicted. He was very strong but could also be very gentle. His eyes were a dark blue. His badge read Barry McNeely – Navy Medic. People called him Bruiser or Mac.

Joe reached Richard Kessler, six feet two, a rangy type of man. A Christian, good to all, but not a man to cross. His specialty was communication, and there was very little he didn't know about communication and computers. His badge read German Intelligence.

Albert Kingsbury – Al to his friends, which were many – was one of New York's finest. He had been with the bomb squad there and served two tours, one in Iraq and one in Afghanistan. His height five feet four inches and he had a slightly rotund build. He and Susie would joke on their height as time went on.

Christopher Wolf was the last to receive his ID badge, which read Army Sniper. Meticulous, patient, and furious when aroused.

"Now that the badges have been passed out, Major Biernacki and Captain LaCoste will leave our august company as they have their own chores to attend to. You will see them again."

Both men rose, said their goodbyes and good lucks, and left.

We will now have our breakfast. The two tables that had been removed were pushed back into place, loaded with food. Two waiters were in attendance to serve them.

"Ah yes, before I forget, from now on you will be known as Shadow Team. You will track together, work together, live together and possibly die together.

You will be as a shadow, slipping in and out – no one will even know you exist."

CHAPTER THIRTY-TWO

While breakfast was being served, the team members met together and talked. They spoke of where they came from and where they were going.

"Well, I'm trying for a new start. Didn't like where I had been and more or less – less being the operational word --- I was talked into joining Alpha." Chris spoke to Susie and Mac.

"I know what you mean," broke Al. "My job was going nowhere in NYPD, except up in little pieces. So when Alpha asked me to volunteer and mentioned some of the benefits, I found it hard to resist."

"I just wanted a change, not much of an upward movement for a woman where I was. This sounded too good to pass up."

"Sounds like all of us came into Alpha with the chance for a change. I also was dead ended and yes, I also thought this job sounded too good to pass up."

"Well Rich – same for me – they said I would be a medic, but cross train in other fields and also learn more of the medical field and go as far as I wanted."

"Well guys," Chris raised his orange juice glass," Here's to Shadow Team. Long life, adventure, and health."

"Here, here, you betcha! Count me in, yes sir," chimed in the team, and all laughed. Chris laughed, "All for one, and one for all."

"All right, all right," Prof Alcorn came in and nodded to the stewards, who rolled away the tables, "Have a seat. Now that breakfast is over, could I have your attention?"

Everyone went to their seats. Breakfast had gone well. The group had intermingled. Biernacki and LaCoste had been introduced as part of the team. Alcorn was pleased that overall, it was a good start.

"Welcome to Alpha, your new home. In the following months, you will work for us and fight for and with your team. Hopefully you will all make it through training. If you don't, there are several more teams taking the same training and will be able to fit in."

"Alpha doesn't leave much to chance, does it?" Al broke out.

"No, it doesn't. We take as few chances as we can to complete the missions, which is good for you – shit happens and if it does, we want to be ready."

"Once again, for those of you who didn't notice it – I was leader here of the Hostage Release Team. I trained at Alpha and served in the field. After several years, because of my unique talents, I was placed into the position to acquaint new people with the workings of Alpha and act as your guide."

He walked slowly in front of the group.

"Alpha is a conglomerate of many large multi-national companies, fighting and working for the survival of the world. We live in dangerous times. There are those who would work singularly, and some together, to gain power and riches – to the detriment of society. We go after these evil sons of bitches who don't give a damn about anyone. Man or woman, law and order, religion, politics, none of those are important to them. We stop them. At the same time, Alpha on the surface exists to help people whenever disaster, disease or devastation exists.

Most of us have been brought up from childhood to adulthood to believe in truth and justice. They do exist, not so much in our children's books, but they do exist. It is our job to keep the faith."

"So, what are we?" asked Chris.

"Yeah, are we some nuts who fight the good fight?" questioned Mac.

"I think what Professor Alcorn is saying," said Susie, "is that someone must speak up for the good people in the world."

"Yes, Susie. That's Alpha. You must be the hammer or the anvil. We chose to be the hammer. However, we will fight fire with fire. We are in this to win for the good guys. If we have to, we will get dirty and will not shrink from a fight. The bad guys always go with the knowledge that we, the good guys, will not go down to their level of fight – that is where they are wrong. Alpha will go to their level, and lower, to beat them."

"But doesn't that make us as bad as them?" Kessler exclaimed.

"No, in our world there is a wrong and right – drugs harming people are bad, terrorists bombing innocents is wrong, slavery in any form should not exist. Dictatorships taking lives should not be allowed. Alpha exists to help, not to hinder."

"So how do we choose bad from good, or what to change or not?"

"I'm glad you asked, Kingsbury. We have a council or group of people that are from the conglomerates that make up Alpha – their job is to receive reports regularly on the world situations. What groups are active, what terrorists are starting to destroy what basically the bad guys are doing. Whenever we can we notify local authorities to the problems but if news gets to the council that – for argument's sake – some nuclear warheads are being brought to use against a country where time is of the essence … we will take the appropriate steps."

We will take the appropriate steps."

"How do we know what or how bad this situation is?"

"Well Rich, I see we are full of good questions today. The information given to the council is looked over by them and given to NATALIE to find analysis."

"I'll bite. What makes Natalie so important?"

"Al, Natalie is a computer, but not just any computer," Alcorn exclaimed, getting more excited. "It is…"

"Excuse me, Professor Alcorn. If you don't mind, could I explain?" The voice was soft, well-modulated and the opaque walls slightly glowed and faded with each syllable of sound.

The team looked at one another, Professor Alcorn spoke with a slight smile, "of course Natalie, please do."

"Thank you. Good morning Christopher, Susie, Richard, Albert, Mac, also to be known as "Shadow Team". I am Natalie – that is to say, I am a Naturally Activated Tactically Analytically Logically Integrated Engine."

CHAPTER THIRTY-THREE

"No offense, Natalie," Wolf spoke up, "But doesn't all that mean is, you're a super computer that is a puzzle?"

"Ah, Mr. Wolf, you have a grasp of the obtuse. I am exactly that, no one who is familiar with me knows exactly how I work except that I do. Let me explain. I am fed in formulations by computer systems all over the world. They collect their information, pass it on to me. I am a greatly improved multi-faceted statistical analysis computer that takes into account millions of factors. I come to a conclusion based on real world scenarios that I feed back to the committee for their final perusal and acceptance."

Kessler spoke up. "I can appreciate all the info gathering and conclusions, etc. – but isn't this like "Big Brother" is watching us? How can we trust you not to screw us over – or take over, for that matter?"

"That is a good point Richard, and part of that is where the enigma lies. I won't do it. I have been programmed with ethics, logic and functions and parameters, and my own self-worth that make me unable to take over, and at the same time, allow me to respond to elements that are harmful to the world or humanity as a whole. After a decision is made, I then select a team, or person – equip them and guide them from the start of the mission to the end. I will be with you to the very end."

CHAPTER THIRTY-FOUR

"Now," went on Natalie, "We have an idea of how Alpha works both covertly and overtly. Overtly we help out wherever we can when a disaster strikes; covertly we crush the bad guys as it were by direct or indirect intervention."

"Okay sounds good, but what're some examples of what you and Alpha do when the shit hits the fan?"

The opaque glass glowed.

"I can, Mr. Wolf, give you several examples of the different situations that have arisen that Alpha has taken a hand in."

"Covertly, we can to go September 24th 2003, when we suggested to the CIA, years earlier than was disclosed, an undertaking that would be in their best interests."

The team hunched forward to listen – spellbound by the computer.

"It was just before dawn when four of the nation's most highly valued terrorist prisoners were brought to Guantanamo Bay, Cuba. Months later they were just as quietly whisked away."

"So what? They come in, they go?"

"The point is Mac, that their transfer allowed the U.S. to interrogate the detainees in CIA "black sites" for two more years without allowing them to speak with attorneys or human rights observers."

"But that's not right, is it?" queried Susie.

The light glowed a little stronger.

"It may not be right in the legal sense of the word, if these individuals were combatants, open fighters as it were, but they were not. They came in as terrorists and therefore, in our eyes, threw away any form of due process."

"Now on March 11, 2011 when Japan, Fukushima to be exact, got hit by a 9.0 quake, tsunami and reactor breakdown – we gave help with tons of foodstuffs, water and man power. We also covertly spoke to Chief Cabinet Secretary Yukio Edano to first tell the people that there was no threat until facts could be uncovered, either yay or nay."

"They immediately placed people in there under great implied risk. We also placed people in there with much better protective gear than they had ... they rushed into the lion's den without thought."

"So why did they do something stupid like that, if we were going in with – according to you -- much better suits?"

"Yes Mac, they did, but the Japanese have such a strong sense of obligation they felt they had to go in there first. This time, we only suggested what to do."

"Now in Libya we covertly told NATO to implement a no fly zone to assist the rebels. We also advised President Obama and the U.N. to take a slow ride in because at first, we did not know the politics of the rebels. Mr. Gaddafi was battling his own people, but the rebels were an unknown."

"Now in Egypt on February 11th, 2011 when the people revolted, we were more assured of who would take over and more or less be friendly to our cause, so we strongly and covertly aided in the overthrow of Hosni Mubarak."

"Okay, all that is interesting, but as the old saying goes, what have you done lately for us? What new thing or act."

"That is a good question Al, and I can answer it in this way. For the past two years, Iran has experimented in nuclear energy. Recently they have been very aggressive, too much so.

The U.S., Israel, and other Arab countries spoke against this experimentation, to no avail.

Then all of a sudden, in January 2012, several nuclear scientists were killed that had a significant position in Iran's nuclear progress. These unfortunate killings have put Iran's nuclear capabilities back several years. That is what Alpha has done for us recently, Al."

"And that, ladies and gentleman, are examples of how Alpha works."

"Thank you, Natalie," interjected Professor Alcorn. We all appreciate your little discourse on Alpha.

"Now people, today's festivities have come to an end."

The group got up and was about to leave when Alcorn broke in. "Tomorrow we will meet here at 0630 –"

"Why so early?"

"Ah yes, Mr. Kessler, good question. Tomorrow you will undergo a small surgical procedure, a small implant likened to a GPS chip. It is quite harmless and you will have nothing to fear. It will take about 45 minutes, and then lunch and explanation."

"Hey Prof – you wouldn't tell us even if did hurt, would you?"

"Why Al, what ever would give you that idea?"

CHAPTER THIRTY-FIVE

Once again, they had all congregated in the conference room.

"So, how are you all doin'?"

"Okay," answered Wolf, "Thanks for asking, Rich."

"Fine, superb," chimed in Sue and Al. "I just want this over and done with. I can handle other people and their injuries, but when it comes to my temple of life, I get a little queasy," spoke up Mac.

"Well, I'm glad to see everyone so bright and cheery this morning," smiled Professor Alcorn as he walked in.

"Like we had a choice."

"Yeah, right."

"Now, now, Rich, Mac – it won't be that bad. In fact, from what Natalie has just informed me, the pain level will be very low."

A low hum was heard, as a small white with gold trim enclosed cart pulled up.

"Now if you all climb in, we'll go to the inpatient section of our hospital. On the way, Natalie will explain the procedure to all of you. Since this will initiate the unity of her and Shadow Team.

When they were all in the cart, it glided off on soft rubber wheels with a slight hum. Translucent light filled the cart, and then pulsed.

"Good morning everyone. I see you're all fine, and although a little apprehensive, very healthy."

"And how would you know?" spoke up Al.

"I've been monitoring, through strategically placed sensors, all of you since you arrived at Alpha. Just to see your reaction to a new environment. You all have done well, except," The light gave off a small pulse, "except for Mac, who has shown a slight elevation in blood pressure."

"You would too, if someone was going to break into your body."

"Ah, Mac. I see a definite clarification is needed to help allay your apprehension about the procedure."

"Yeah, that would be a good idea -- not that I'm worried about it, mind you."

"Yes, I understand, Rich. Well, to explain. We are going to the inpatient wing at Alpha Hospital. There, under a very mild local anesthetic, a small, very powerful microchip with a titanium alloy shell will be implanted into your non-dominant underarm. It is placed in this location because it is less prone to injury."

"Why all the protection, why do we need it?" The light pulsed a little darker.

"Because, Mr. Wolf, that chip will connect you, all of you, to me – the Shadow Team will be the Shadow Team because of this chip. This chip will be the life or death of all of you. The Shadow Team will exist, or not exist, because of it."

CHAPTER THIRTY-SIX

"What do you mean connected?" spoke Rich.

"What's life and death? What the hell are you talking about?"

Al rose, slightly agitated. At that moment the cart came to a stop, along with Al.

"Ah, ladies and gentlemen, we have arrived. Now if you'll follow me we will do this as painlessly and quickly as possible. Over breakfast is a more civilized atmosphere. All your questions will be answered – concerning the chip, that is."

They were ushered down a short hallway into a typical hospital consisting of a desk, several chairs, a couch, and end tables. The receptionist glanced up and smiled at Professor Alcorn.

"Hello Professor. I see you have your team today. Are they ready?"

"Janie, they're biting at the bit and rarin' to go."

The team looked at each other. Mac looked at Jane – "I'm not nervous, I'm scared shitless about someone touching this body."

Jane batted her eyes at Mac.

"Well a big strong man like you shouldn't let a little ole procedure like this bother you. It really doesn't hurt."

"Well thanks, Jane," broke in Al sarcastically, "that makes me feel a whole lot better."

"I'll ring for Eva, she'll be your head nurse and will guide you all through the procedure."

"Eva, they're here."

"Okay Jane, I'll be right there," spoke a lightly moderate voice with just a hint of a Southern inflection.

"She'll be right here."

At that moment the door to the left of the desk opened and in walked a dusky, dark haired young nurse in a light blue uniform, and on her rather robust chest was her name tag – Eva McCante, RN, SAA.

"Hello everyone, this will be a quick and relatively painless procedure, taking ..."

"Yeah, yeah, we know it will be over before we know it ..." grimaced Mac.

"Right, it will take roughly ten minutes and then Professor Alcorn will take you to breakfast and explain all."

Professor Alcorn nodded in agreement.

"Now, please come with me and we'll get started."

The team followed Eva and Alcorn, who walked at a brisk pace through a set of double doors. Wolf noticed inside placed side by side were five tables, each one having a different colored covering. The walls were tan with a touch of blue.

"Nice," said Wolf, "It leaves you with a quiet feeling."

"Yes," Eva said, "and as you came through those doors a slight mist was sprayed on you. It is an aerosol anesthetic we use for our less invasive procedures."

"That's why we came in as a group and you and the Professor were ahead of us," declared Sue.

"You got it. You should feel calm, slightly mellow with no anxiety."

"I don't know about the rest of you, but I am definitely calm," giggled Mac.

The team all laughed at such a big man giggling, and feeling no pain themselves. They knew of his fear but also knew nothing would stop him from completing the mission.

"All right, all right," Eva broke in. Take a colored table and we'll begin.

The people chose their tables, and made themselves comfortable while the technicians came in, two to a small push cart, and sat themselves at each table.

"Now raise your dominant arm, the one you use the most." The technician checked their charts and moved accordingly to the opposite arm.

"Now, under your arm near the crease there will be placed a chip. It will be injected into the muscle. An anesthetic will be injected with the chip and you will only feel a pinprick."

The room grew silent then.

"This is alright Eva," exclaimed Rich, "No problem."

"That's it people, it's over."

"That's it? It's over, over – just like that?"

"Yes Mac, just like that. It's over."

"I think," Professor Alcorn broke in, "That you have all relearned a valuable lesson today – try not to over think what is going to happen. Approach it, but don't let it carry you away. Now if you'll follow me back to the cart, we'll get breakfast. I'm sure you're dying to eat."

Just as they were going through the office to the cart – the lighting started to pulse – Natalie's voice could be heard.

"Attention, attention to all personnel. Thanks to information we gathered and passed on to the U.S. Government and President Obama – Osama Bin Laden has been captured and killed by Seal Team 6, a joint combination of services repelling into his compound. Once again," and the light pulsed stronger, "Osama Bin Laden is dead."

The Shadow Team looked at each other, smiled and then shouted and hugged.

"All right people – relax, get it together. Today you have had a firsthand look at what Alpha does. Aren't you all glad you joined?"

CHAPTER THIRTY-SEVEN

Wolf wiped his mouth and took another sip of coffee. Al and Sue were talking about Bin Laden. Mac and Rich were going over the procedure and how they would never worry about procedures again – until the next time.

"All right people, let's quiet down. Natalie is now going to explain the chip – what it is and its use."

Once again the pulsing light, followed by a low well-modulated voice – Natalie was here.

"I'm glad to see you all survived and are on the way to recovery."

"I'm glad to see you can joke about it Natalie, personally I was scared."

"As stated before I had all of you under surveillance and none of you, including you Mac, were in any danger, either physically or mentally. As far as the joke, I was just stating an observation."

"Now as to the chip under your arm."

"Now comes the good stuff – the nitty-gritty."

"Yes Al, you're quite right. Now if you'll listen … "

"All right Prof, you got me, "Al raised his arm, "I'll be quiet."

The wall light pulsed.

"Now the chip was placed under your less dominant arm because it is not as easily accessible to damage say, if you were fighting. The chip is powered by the chemical processes of your body, including the sweat glands which use very minute flicks of electricity."

"You mean our sweat and the reaction of that powers the chip?"

"Yes, Mr. Wolf, exactly. It is a normal function that makes the chip non-recognizable by any surveillance device."

"As for the chip itself, it has several functions. When activated you become invisible to any satellite tracking systems, infrared systems, any radar system that exists today. You cause no interference at all. One of these devices, a camera, could be right next to you and no heat, picture or shape is registered."

"You mean we're invisible?"

"For all intents and purposes, to any of those machines, you do not exist. There is no register of you being there. You are just normal background activity."

"Also, you will have a uniform that is so revolutionary only Alpha has it. It is a combination of these discoveries."

"One, as I mentioned before, the chemical reaction which powers the chip. Two, everything we do generates power – about 1 watt per breath, 70 watts per step. Michael McAlpine of Princeton University and his group found out how to turn locomotion into power by embedding piezoelectric crystals into a flexible biocompatible rubberlike material, that when bent, allows the crystals to produce energy. This will generate power for your walkies, for the chip, and remain neutral to any observations.

Now couple that with two other findings – one is a spray on fabric incorporating this rubber. The Biotech company Fabrican has developed a way to bond and liquefy fibers onto a body."

"Like our rubber suit."

"Yes Rich, the rubber and spray go on together along with a covering called X-Flex which is to be used as a wallpaper to stop a building from collapsing from lethal force. It's a Kevlar-like material that combined with our materials and elastic polymer wrap – becomes stronger than any force that attacks it."

"So we have a super suit that makes us invisible, strong and resistant to any tracking or surveillance device that exists."

"Yes Mac, and the chip has two more functions. It connects to me, so during any mission I am there with you to offer any assistance, and you can also communicate with me at will."

"So we can speak to you out loud or use the chip as a radio and keep silent, by what 'using our thoughts'?"

"Exactly, Mr. Wolf. In fact, for the last hour that's exactly what you've been doing, and I might add, you can speak to each other the same way. This is why you are the 'Shadow Team'."

"You are all shadows moving along the ground, unknown and unseen, to kill the enemy."

CHAPTER THIRTY-EIGHT

The wind was whistling, sighing, slipping its way under the doors into his apartment. The rain pounding against the window, demanding to get in.

Wolf woke, listening, smiling. He loved this weather – nature unleashed, trying to get man to acquiesce to its power. Man fought. This was the struggle Wolf loved.

Today, the team was going on tour. Taken around Alpha to finally see what this place was all about. The wind continued. He went to dress.

He arrived at the lounge area, as people had come to call it. His team was there.

"Ah, my team, it has a nice ring to it but a little daunting – I will have to get used to this." Everyone said hello. "Morning, how're you doing?"

They were all getting coffee, juices – when a man, about five foot-seven built like a miniature sumo wrestler, walked in. He was bald, had a beautiful smile, with a nice chuckle and the coldest, glacier blue eyes Wolf had ever seen.

"Well people – and you are and will be my people, for training and mission direction. My name is Josiah Jones. I am a former bounty hunter, so my attitude will be a trifle unorthodox, as befitting that position. You will treat me with respect, and I will treat you – well, we'll see how I treat you."

"Now, it's my understanding you all have had the chip implanted. However, for this period of training, and until I notify you, we will speak normally … "

"Excuse me, Mr. Jones? When and or where does this implant or whatever you call it, come into play?"

"Good question."

"Natalie, could you please inform Richard as to our chip?"

The familiar light came on, pulsed.

"Thank you, Richard. The chip's function of telecommunication will come into play on the occasions when we are training, and on an actual mission."

"You mean us, the team?"

"No, Mac, I mean the team, and me. We will communicate with each … "

"Thank you, Natalie, for the information. We'll go into the other ramifications in the near future. For now, we have a lot to do, and we have to go."

"Of course, Josiah. I understand." The light pulsed and slowly faded.

"All right, Shadow, let's be on our way. We'll now go through Alpha, visiting the various locations in which you will train for your missions, whatever they might be. You will train in postures such as weapons, communications, hand to hand and other tools of the trade."

"We will also – if time allows – make an actual replica of what your mission will be, so you will be better prepared to handle it."

"Not to be an alarmist, but how many times does this work out for us, given we have the time?"

"Ah, Susie, is it?"

"Yes, it is."

"Well, it works out more times than not."

"Ah, I sense the big "If" coming into play. My ole' uncle Dick used to say "If" "stands alone." Al said with raised eyebrows and imitation cigar in his mouth, ala Groucho Marx.

"Yes, right," Josiah continued, "If … we are warned in time, if the conditions are correct, it will work. You are the Shadow Team. Your training is intense. You will work together like a well-oiled machine. With Natalie's guidance, you can go if necessary with little or no notice. She will be able to furnish you with overall information and guidance through the chip. The chip can also furnish actual pictures to you that you will see."

"So we go in on a mission and hope for the best, expect the worst, and take anything we can get."

"Not exactly, Mac," Natalie broke in, "It is more on a seventy-seven and a third percentile of success over a normal forty-three percent success rate." The light pulsed. "You have a better chance of living than of dying."

"Thank you, Natalie, for your cheerful stats. And now, without further ado, we'll continue our tour."

CHAPTER THIRTY-NINE

The ride in the cart was uneventful. Josiah stopped the cart at one of several elevators.

"We'll be going down to the training levels, and we'll reach bottom in approximately fifteen seconds for level one."

"Are we going to the fifth gate of hell?"

"Not quite Al, although at times you'll think so."

The doors opened. Josiah drove the cart in. It was a massive elevator with front and back openings.

"Down, please."

"Yes, Mr. Jones. The training level, Mr. Jones?"

"No, first we'll go to the offices and supply areas, then training."

"Very good, Mr. Jones."

The elevators descended rapidly, but with little or no sense of speed. A chime sounded, the doors opened smoothly, and Josiah drove the cart out onto a small blacktop road. They went about a quarter of a mile, and Jones pulled over and parked. They got out and followed Josiah to what looked like a huge steel door about twelve feet tall and seven feet wide. He stood in front of the door and a light pulsed over him.

"Welcome, Mr. Jones. Are you and Shadow Team going for the look around?"

"Yes we are, Stella, and as we go in please put their chips into the memory banks and allow them full access to any level."

"Yes, Josiah, as they pass through they'll be collected."

The pulse faded. The door opened smoothly, slowly. The door, five feet thick, moved silently. The largeness impressed Wolf and the team.

"Nice," whistled Al, "I don't think this door can be blown very easily," appraising the thickness of the door.

"I definitely know this is the fifth circle of hell. Maybe sixth, no doubt about it," joked Mac.

"Please, go into the waiting room. The door will close, the inner door will then open," spoke Stella.

"Josiah."

"Yes, Mr. Wolf?"

"This is well calculated to keep us in suspense."

"Not quite, but what's wrong with a little suspense while getting there? Anticipation, Mr. Wolf, anticipation."

The group filed in and the door shut. A glow filled the room, preceded by a slight tingle to the flesh. Then the inner door slowly opened.

As the team filed out, there was a small well lit street, going for what seemed like forever in both directions. Josiah directed them to another cart.

"First we'll go to the right, and we'll see storage, enter supply and equipment, and uniform dispersal."

The cart rolled along, passing by huge fenced in areas marked by signs as emergency ration, water, clothes, medical equipment, and so on. They stopped by what looked like a small lake stretching into the distance. Looking down was a little beach with a motor boat on it.

"This is our water supply. We have all sorts of emergency rations, but for our regular needs, the lake fulfills our needs."

"This is like 'Journey to the Center of the Earth', it's unreal."

"Mr. Wolf, you don't know the half of it. This is only a small part. Now we'll go to the desert and mountain training area."

The team got into the cart, Josiah turned it around and headed back.

They passed offices brightly lit with bold letters in gold describing who or what was inside. Defense, supply, logistics, communication. They passed crossroads where other offices existed.

"So far, this is just like one big school – a self-sufficient, self-sustaining school."

"Exactly, Susie. It is. It is made in some aspects to resemble a school, so as to create in the trainee a comfort zone. People learn more when they're comfortable."

"I'm impressed – it's fascinating."

"Rich, you have yet to be truly fascinated," smiled Josiah.

"Ah, here we are. Our first real mock-up training station."

The sign on the door read Desert and Mountain Training Replica. The sign beneath it said "Please be careful" with a smiley face.

They entered into an office area filled with people and arrays of desks and machines. Jones nodded to some and greeted others.

"This resembles a NASA mock-up area," quipped Rich.

They continued through the office, to a hallway.

"When we go around this bend, you will come to an observation level where you will look out and see around two and a half miles of desert and mountain background."

The first thing they felt was the heat, it crept up on them. They rounded the corner and the wind and sun with the heat hit them, along with the view.

"My God, we landed in Pellucidar."

"I don't believe this."

"What the hell – is this real?"

"Jesus."

"I am definitely impressed!"

"I see you're all amazed. You should be. This is our desert and mountain training site. It is not only like the real thing, it is the real thing. Out there is a desert in all its glory, and the mountains with crags and precipices. It's on a smaller scale, but still just as lethal and dangerous as the ones above us. The training in the heat is hard and difficult."

"The only difference here is – this is a secret facility. You can live and die here, and no one would ever know."

CHAPTER FORTY

The sun, or what passed for it, had been beating down on Shadow Team for the past three days. Heat waves rolled over the sand, mirages formed pools of water that weren't there. The Shadow Team walked spritely along, encased inside of their newly acquired protection suits. They were being helped along the way with directions from Natalie and speaking freely to her and each other, due to their chips.

Everything was beautiful, delightful. That would end in about ten minutes.

"Shadow Team, Wolf, you others, over ... "

"Yes Jones, what is it?" queried Wolf.

"Gotcha, Jonesy."

"What's up, Boss?"

"Hear you."

"Loud and clear."

"All right, enough. I'm breaking protocol because I want you all to know that in ten minutes, your suits will deactivate ... "

"What?"

"C'mon!"

"Gonna do what?"

"Quiet. Listen. In ten minutes, your suits and chips will be gone. They will cease to function. You will be, for all intents and purposes, on your own. You will get back to the portal as soon as you can. Wolf, take your team. Don't forget, people, this is real. You can die out there. Good luck."

Silence, nothing, just a little breathing in the wind. They looked at each other. "Well, we're in the shit now," Susie blurted.

"Hey, we can make it. We got out here, didn't we?"

"Yes Rich, we got out here, but that was with the suit and Natalie, now we go back without … "

"Hey, hey guys," spoke up Wolf. "Mac, we did get out here, and let's face it folks, this is not the hardest problem we have ever faced. Look – no one's shooting at us, we have enough water and food tables to sustain us for several days, so let's not go crazy. Now take a small drink of water, eat a couple of tablets, and let's go. We have nothing to worry about. It'll be a cake walk."

"Oh yeah," exclaimed Mac, "Our cake just went flat, look over there."

The team looked over to where Mac was pointing – a huge cloud of dust was coming their way. It rose up and out, the wind with a loud mournful wail crept closer, coming in on them.

"Face plates down, collar up, make as little space as you can to keep out sand particles," spoke Wolf in a loud voice. "Now take this rope, pass it through that big grommet in your belt, and keep it about five foot intervals. That way we'll keep close, but not fall over each other. We'll walk to that overhang we passed about a quarter of a mile back, hunker down until the storm passes.

"Okay Wolf!" yelled Mac. Rose and Al gave the thumbs down and smiled at one another. Wolf noticed it and smiled. Rich nodded, and away they went.

The storm hit them hard. The roar of the wind, the sand flying through the air, creeping into spaces, pores, like little insidious beings intent to get you, devour you. Each person felt a bit numb, but Shadow Team was good. They had faith in each other.

"We'll pull through," thought Wolf, "My guys are tough."

All of a sudden there was a tremendous pull on the rope, pulling Wolf back. He looked back and saw Mac and Al yelling and gesturing through the storm, but to no avail.

He made his way through the storm to them. They yelled, but the wind and sand rose to a piercing roar. They pointed back to Rich, who was bent over and looked like he had a fish at the end of his line. They staggered back, hauling their rope to shorten it.

They got to Rich, and he pointed down a little hill in which he was standing, to Susie below. She had stepped out of line and broke through what had appeared to be solid sand, but was really very fine shifting, moving sand that resembled quicksand.

She moved and sunk deeper and deeper. The rope held her up.

Immediately, the men saw their predicament and grabbed the shorter rope and pulled. They pulled hard, but so did the sand. They pulled strong, but so did the sand. They grunted through the howling wind, yelled and pulled, then a release, a small vibration in the rope. The wind howled in anger, the sand tore into them. Susie screamed and with that scream, out she popped from the hole like a cork out of a bottle.

The team fell back, thoughts jumbled.

"Jesus, she's out!"

"Thank God."

"Good ol' Shadow, knew we could do it."

"That's my Wolf."

"Thank you guys, I'm glad you're mine."

The team made their way back to the overhang and collapsed. They snuggled closer together and fell asleep.

The wind howled, moaned, and then silence.

CHAPTER FORTY-ONE

Wolf woke up to a slight buzzing in his head, which soon became a little louder. Then the voice of Jonah broke in, and the buzzing stopped.

"Attention Shadow Team – wake up, rise and shine. Wolf get everyone up, we just got a new mission that is right up your alley. It's all yours."

"Wolf over, this is fast isn't it? Not that I mind, but how do we stand on training?"

"Minor factor."

"Yeah," broke in Al. "Sure."

"As I was saying – Natalie, as you know, has been continually monitoring all of you. Your physical and mental condition and well-being. According to her, you are all well suited (pardon the pun) and anything you lack is minor. The invincibility suits and chips you have, give you more than the average percentile of success. Natalie's words, not mine."

"When do we go?"

"Where do we go?"

"How do we go?"

"What's the mission?"

"All right people, all right. Jones will explain, right Jones?"

"Quite right, Wolf. All your questions will be answered when you arrive back at base."

"The sooner the better."

"Right again, Wolf. A chopper is being sent as we speak and your friends Biernacki and LaCoste will be your pilots. In fact they should be here in about five, four, three, two … now!"

A large, quiet chopper landed, kicking up dust. The group lowered their heads as the rotors slowed down. When they looked up, on the front of the chopper nose was painted a mouth with shark's teeth. The chopper was dark and would show no reflection on any radar screens. The blades stopped. A door opened and out stepped LaCoste, a smile on his face, waving to the group.

The group waved back and started moving forward towards the chopper, following Wolf.

"How you guys doin'? All right I hope. Sorry to have to cut your little walk in the sun short, but duty calls and rumor has it it's one hell of a mission.

The group tittered and grinned.

"I knew it wouldn't last long, and we would be doing … "

"Sure, sure," grinned Rich, slapping Mac on the back, "You saw it all."

"Well it sure as hell beats baking in the sun."

"Right Al, it does, or whatever the sun is here," exclaimed Susie.

"All right people, let's go. Into the chopper and buckle in, we have an appointment."

"Right you are, Wolf me boy, the Biernacki and I will get you there as fast as possible for your exciting new adventure."

The team climbed aboard, sat and strapped in. The blades started rotating faster and faster like a beast ready to pounce.

Biernacki released the collective lever, the helicopter shot straight up and forward. The team was pushed down into their seats and just as suddenly pushed back into their seats.

The desert was whipping by beneath their feet.

Biernacki came over the headphones. "Hope the takeoff didn't bother you. We realize it wasn't the normal lift off of a chopper, but we have to get to Alpha in a hurry. From what I understand they want to brief you and have you take off by 2300 hrs tonight."

"No sir. You didn't bother us a bit. I just left my stomach and balls on the floor."

"Now, now, Mac. It wasn't that bad," laughed LaCoste. "Besides, it's better than walking, isn't it?" There was a large groan from the group.

The trip lasted for about twenty minutes. Alpha came into view, big and white. Biernacki landed the ship, cut the power, opened the door.

"Everybody out. Okay now, follow me."

He led them over to a large cart, got in. They all followed.

"Okay guys," said Al. "Here comes the last gate of hell, where we all suffer."

Wolf looked at him, "Al, you may not be wrong."

CHAPTER FORTY-TWO

They entered Alpha, where a man about five foot seven, thinning brown hair, bright eyes and a very Lincolnesque face welcomed them.

"Howdy, my name is Mucci. Most people call me Muckeye. I'm going to be your liaison for this mission. If for some reason Natalie and you guys break off communications, then hopefully I will be there to help you. If not, then you're on your own. Now, if you'll follow me, we'll go to the in briefing room and find out from Natalie where we'll be going."

"You're coming with us?"

"Mr. Wolf, I'll be here."

"Okay MacDuff, lead on."

"It's Muckeye."

"Right, lead on Muckeye," smiled Al, making a sweeping motion with his arm.

"Oh yeah – here we go."

"This is kind of fun."

Everyone looked at Susie, then laughed.

"Right, let's go. We're with you, Muckeye," motioned Wolf.

"Okay, we'll take this elevator to the fifteenth floor, get off, take a right, and the in briefing room will be on your left, about four doors down."

In a matter of seconds, the elevator arrived on the fifteenth floor. Everyone got out, moved to the right, down the hall. Muckeye pointed to a door on the left with a sign over it describing it as Briefing Room Number Three.

Muckeye opened the door, ushered the group in. As they entered, they saw a group of nine very plush looking reclining chairs in a half-circle. They saw on the walls pictures, photos, paintings, various objects which made them feel completely at ease, comfortable, secure. The walls pulsed with a soft glow, Natalie's voice came to them.

"Thank you all for coming. Now if you'll take a seat, we'll begin the briefing. When you all walked in, I went into your files and pulled out memories, close enough for you to recognize, to make you feel secure. It is a little bit like comfort food, but for the mind, which affected your sense of well-being. You can now sit down, and we'll begin."

"I'm fine," smiled Al, "Let's go."

"Go ahead," saluted Mac.

"Fire when ready, Gridley," said Rich.

"Once again people, let's relax – but not too much – and let Natalie explain what's going to happen."

"You go, Wolf," smiled Susie, giving Wolf the okay signal with her hand.

"As I was saying, from this point on you will be receiving all information through your chip. That information from the chip will then be transmitted to appropriate centers of your brain, as soon as I send it. Now sit back, relax, and I'll switch to your chips."

"This is just like the old Outer Limits show," spoke up Al.

"Yeah, do not adjust your set … "

"Excuse me, Richard, may I continue?" Richard moved back and into the chair.

"Go ahead, Natalie, we're all yours."

"Thank you, Mr. Wolf."

Muckeye observed the give and take between the team and Natalie, and was pleased. Biernacki and LaCoste had signaled him with a salute. That was good. These people would have to work together better than any team would have to. They would have to work as one. Fight as one. Maneuver and think as one. They would soon find out. If this did not happen, Alpha would be looking for a new Shadow Team.

CHAPTER FORTY-THREE

The team sat back as Natalie took over.

Pictures flashed through their minds. Atomic bombs exploding with a blinding light as the mushroom cloud rose into the sky. Winds of hurricane force rushing along the ground at a hundred and fifty miles an hour, bringing nova like heat with it. Blowing to pieces, shattering, destroying anything in its way. Hell come to earth. People here one second, vapor the next. Flesh igniting, burning into human candles. Shadows on walls, where hopes, dreams and life used to be. Patients in hospitals with black, burned skin. Hair pulling out, bald. Blood coming from their bodies, hemorrhaging inside. Dying a horrible death. Death is terrible, but this is terrifying. Susie gasped.

Soldiers walking along a deserted street, all of a sudden some start to fall. One soldier notices, "Masks, masks!" All soldiers reach for their masks as they are trained to do, but it is too late. They start foaming at the mouth, grab their throats, they can't breathe. Blood seeps from their skin, eyes, tears of blood. Screams echo, "Mother, mother!" Writhing on the ground, bowels opening, voiding, piss flows. Blisters form on the men inside and out, bursting, filling lungs, drowning some with their own fluids. Soon all is quiet. Nothing moves, everyone is dead.

A rabbit, its claw held by hands with heavy rubber gloves. A pin touched to the claw, the pinpoint had been touched to a brownish liquid, then the tip blowtorched. The tip glowing red. Touched to the claw one of the hardest, most non-porous substances on any animal. X-unknown a new bacteria is introduced. It gave its introductions to the rabbit. The rabbit collapsed and died, hemorrhaging, convulsing and blind. Time; a little under ten seconds. Wolf recoiled from the vivid images.

"You have just seen the effects of atomic and chemical attacks. They are deadly and with atomics, can take a while; with chemical, a short time. A neutron bomb kills, but only people. They can be selective.

Now bacterial is the deadliest form of the three. It is insidious, you can't see, feel, or smell it. The testing of it comes from victims who are dying or dead. Dead is more helpful, as an autopsy can be performed and get to the root cause of the death.

Now imagine a vector, which is the carrier, so deadly it attacks a living host, disables it. Destroys its immune system, causes failure of major organs, leading to internal hemorrhaging and then when the heart dies, the virus dies."

"So if the host dies and the virus dies, then it can't spread. Right?"

"Very good, Mac," the light pulsed, "If unfortunately, wrong. This particular vector spreads very easily through the air with great rapidity and while attacking its host, is widespread to others."

"This sounds like an end of the world type vector. It's not out there, is it? Or is it? Is that why we're here, Natalie? Is this monster out there?"

CHAPTER FORTY-FOUR

"No, Mr. Wolf, this monster is not out there … yet. It does exist, but is buried deep in an underground facility called "Mattabassett." An ultra-secret research laboratory owned and run by Alpha. Its reason for existence is to find antidotes for the most deadly and terrifying substances we have."

"Okay, not good good stuff, but what does that have to do with us?"

"Ah Rich, yes. A few months ago, a medical conference took place in Switzerland with various heads and their assistants attending. It was held under strict control, to discuss reactors, bacteria, viruses and ways to destroy them, so none could ever get out and destroy the world.

I was observing the conference under the most strict protocol required for such meetings. In this case, total all out surveillance, audio, video, satellite. You name it, we had it." The light pulsed. "The exquisite part of all this was no one had any idea they were being monitored, which is how we found out what was going to happen at Mattabassett. I will continue giving you audio, visual and reality imprints throughout your chip so you can better understand the severity of the situation. This narrative will have a ninety-nine percent accuracy."

"What you're saying Natalie, is you're telling us another story like the previous descriptions, to make it more palatable for our minds to comprehend and the other one percent chance of accuracy is due to all the various spying procedures used."

"Bravo, Mr. Wolf, exactly."

"So we should sit back and you should begin?"

"Right again, Al. Let's do that. I'll begin."

"The Mattabassett project is ours, fully funded and run by Alpha. It deals with the discovery of reactors and bacteria that is carried by them, and hopefully their antidote. The person in charge of Mattabassett is Helen Russo, a large brunette, oval face, wears very red lipstick, speaks with a Boston accent and is a lesbian. We do not care about any of these factors due to changes in our society, as they are not pertinent to her running this facility. She is a graduate of MIT and has ten years work at Atlanta Disease Control.

Unfortunately when attending this conference she was approached, seduced and won over by a Karen Lipscome whose childhood was less than desirable, and because of violations perpetrated against her by her family, she has no liking for human beings. She did however, inherit her money and position by her former husband Paul, a diminutive man who was always trying to prove himself. He made lots and lots of money through the selling of anything to anybody for a large profit.

You wanted it, he got it. He and Karen got along famously – he died and she became heir apparent to the throne.

As close as we can understand, Karen went to this conference, approached Helen Russo and seduced her. To ensure her acquiescence, she produced photos of their tryst and promptly burned them, and informed Helen that if she looked into a certain bank account that was in her name, she would find the sum of ten million dollars with the addition of another fifteen million to be paid upon the receiving of certain specimens and papers coming out of Mattabassett.

Helen was taken by surprise, but as Karen was performing cunnilingus on her and making her come off, she very vocally agreed to the deal."

CHAPTER FORTY-FIVE

"So where does that leave us and why bring us in?"

"There was a slight glitch in the reporting and by the time we found out, Helen had gone back to Mattabassett. As soon as she got there, life sign readings started dropping off until there were only two."

"You mean that everyone in Mattabassett is dead but two people?"

"Right Mac, two people."

"Helen and who?"

"Good question Al, as this picture shows a woman strongly resembling Karen Lipscome was admitted to Mattabassett one day before the signals started fading."

"So she and Karen are there and doing what – "

"Well they are there getting together samples and papers and are almost on the way out."

"So why or how did it take this long to find out – with all your setups and satellites and whatever?"

"Uh, yes, well, Mr. Wolf, to be honest that glitch I mentioned was the replaying of life signs and movement on a loop that was fed back to us over and over again. Because this was on forty-eight hour turnaround for films, several days went by before this was noticed and pinpointed to Mattabassett."

"So now what? We go in to this, I am assuming practically impenetrable fortress, and take them out? Why not blow them up? End it."

"I wish we could, Wolf, but it won't work – Mattabassett is a mile and a half down with two outlets, closely guarded and booby trapped."

"Okay so wait until they come out, since they don't know we know they're there, and get them."

"That is a good idea, except Susie, if they are taken and something happens to the material they are taking out and it escapes in the air, quite a lot of us won't be seeing, shall we say, the next day."

"Okay so how do we get to them? According to you, they're buried a mile beneath the surface in a mountain – how do we get in?"

CHAPTER FORTY-SIX

The light pulsed rather heavily.

"We found, that is my resources and I found, that in the very early eighteen hundreds a silver mine was located in that same mountain. Now the records, deeds, plans of that excavation were lost for over two hundred years. Only because of this event happening did research start and reach its full zenith that we found out about this mine."

"In other words, you screwed up, got scared, overturned every rock you could and found out about this secret buried silver mine."

The light pulsed, "Right Mac."

"Okay, so what do we do?"

"What you or me are going to do is a high altitude jump – from about six miles up with your suits, and special filters. You'll be able to jump and fall straight down to within a hundred feet of the tunnel entrance.

Any devices they have to spot any intruders into Mattabassett will be nullified. To further enhance lack of detection, suits are on full, and a time loop, audio-visual tape will be played so that nothing will be picked up. Everything will be same old same old. Except Shadow team will be on the ground."

CHAPTER FORTY-SEVEN

Biernacki and LaCoste flew the team to an Alpha airport located twenty miles from the main building.

It was disguised as a private airport that several corporations in the nearby area used. State of the line radar was in use, as well as electronics that could land a plane by itself with no pilot if necessary. They landed a quarter of a mile away from a Boeing C-17 Globemaster III.

Biernacki and LaCoster got out of the chopper and motioned all to follow them.

Inside there were net seats where the men were led to and stopped.

"All right guys, there are the seats you'll use, you'll find what they call an MC-4 parachute on each seat."

"Right," chimed in LaCoste, "That parachute is specifically designed for HALO jumps, they function reliably in all conditions found on Alpha missions."

Wolf put on his chute and started to help his teammates with theirs.

"Hey not so close with the hands," Al smiled.

"No problem, besides, Susie is the one I want."

"Now you tell me Wolf, when we're here and going on a mission."

Wolf shrugged. "What can I say, I'm bashful."

Mac winked at Rich, "Isn't that the way. Boy meets girl, boy likes girl, then he tells her on their first HALO jump together. How touching."

"Okay, everybody in? Check each other out, make sure their chutes are secure."

The team members groped and pulled the straps and harnesses on each other's chutes.

"Okay, everyone is good," announced Wolf, having been giving the go ahead by his team.

"You all have your Gerber knife and your Cold automatic fitted for .22 magnum shells with hollow point. It has a little extra kick, which makes it feel like you were hit by a .45 hollow point."

"Shades of Dirty Harry, LaCoste with this suit and weapons. I feel invincible."

"Not quite, Mac, but you're able enough to put anyone down that gets in your way."

"Now if you'll all sit down, there is an oxygen mask on the side of your chute. It is connected to the special cartridge bottle that is also attached. Put on your masks now. On your belt is a blue button, please push it now." Immediately the team could feel the oxygen cross their faces and into their lungs.

"This oxygen, combined with special gases, is to get your body saturated to perform to its utmost potential. You'll be in free fall for up to about two minutes, and your altitudes will be at thirty-thousand feet, a thousand feet higher than Mount Everest. That's six miles above the earth's crust, at a minus ten degree. Without a mask you would black out from lack of oxygen in about thirty seconds, resulting in brain damage from hypoxia. Hence your suits, masks, and oxygen," continued Biernacki.

"You're in the troposphere, and if you should open your chute it would explode and you would plummet to earth in a confetti cone, the air being so thin that you would fall twice terminal velocity. This is a very bad altitude. Now LaCoste and I will go forward and get this mission started."

"By the way guys," broke in LaCoste, "It's going to be another unrestricted take off like the one we did in the chopper, pick-up off the desert floor. Only this time we have four Pratt & Whitney turbofan jet engines. Each engine generates forty thousand pounds of thrust. It will be a fun ride. We'll be over our target in about an hour and twenty minutes."

"Good luck and God speed, come back."

They moved and went forward.

CHAPTER FORTY-EIGHT

"Is everyone comfy? I hope so." Natalie's voice filled their minds.

"Major Biernacki and Mr. LaCoste seem to have an excellent grasp of the situation, and filled you in quite nicely as to the mechanics of the mission."

"Yeah, they did, but when we're over target what happens?"

"Good question, Al."

Al looked startled ... he didn't talk, he thought and got answered. The others looked at Al, some surprised.

"Christ, it works!"

"He didn't open his mouth."

"Hey, I can hear him and you guys – this is weird, cool but weird."

"This is new, people, so we're going to have to be careful in our processes. Try to take your time talking or thinking, don't jumble up thoughts together."

"Good thinking Mr. Wolf, but not to worry the chips are fitted with a great many little plusses which unfortunately we're not able to go into because of our lack of time due to this mission."

"Your thoughts won't get jumbled, there is a delay of about one millionth of a second so that everyone's thoughts and words can be understood, but not jumbled. So although you'll all speak at the same time, your thoughts will come through singularly."

"Outstanding, I am so happy we can all talk at once and not be messed up."

"C'mon Rich lighten up, Natalie did us a favor. Now we can all talk at once and everyone will be understood."

"Thank you Al, for your very fundamental insight."

There was a huge rumbling, the plane shook, the air moved, the plane moved down the runway faster and faster, then the break off of earth. They were off into the deep black sky.

CHAPTER FORTY-NINE

"All right, we'll be over the drop zone in just five minutes. Wake up and listen up, here's a few fundamentals.

We are coming in at about thirty thousand feet at this altitude. With the coating and signal abating lasers we have aboard, we are invisible even to Mattabassett. Even if we weren't at this altitude, a plane is just a spec above the clouds. On radar we look just like a commercial flight if we're noticed at all, which we won't be.

Now your chutes will open with enough time to get you down and within a thousand feet of the mine opening.

When the back ramp opens you'll get up, walk to the back of the plane, go to the edge and drop off. When you're out, act like you're lying down with your hands in a hold up position …"

"What the hell is that?"

"That, Al, is like when as a kid you played cowboys and you said 'hold 'em up' you put your hands up."

"Correct, Wolf, and spread your legs a little, this will create a stable platform as the wind goes hurtling about you."

Time went by, each person living with their thoughts.

Wolf thinking about Alice and how if long ago she had lived, everything he had done to this point would never have been executed.

Al was glad he was out of the humdrum of the New York Police Department. Not that he didn't like it, but he was going nowhere, at least now he was going somewhere. "Yeah, out of this plane at thirty thousand feet."

Susie was happy, she liked her job and was glad it wasn't the typical nine to five bullshit.

Mac got to do more medical work here than if he were in civilian life.

Rich didn't care, communications was communications, although he had more sophisticated toys to play with at Alpha.

A thought, voice broke into their minds.

"We are approaching the drop zone. Your suits are activated, oxygen has been circulating in your body. A red light will go on, the platform door will open. When a green light comes on you will walk to the platform and continue to walk right off, hitting the air. Assume the hands up position. You will free fall for about two minutes, then your chute will automatically deploy."

"What if it doesn't?"

"You have a ring, bright orange in front. Pull it out and it will open, Al."

"When you land you'll be about a thousand feet near the opening of that mine."

A red light came on, Shadow Team was ready. The platform door started to open. There was nothing there but blackness. A green light came on, a low command like voice sounded in their heads, "Go, Go!"

They walked to the edge of the platform and went out.

The wind hit them, the blackness enveloped them, they moved into the position and fell. They were going down, down. To what?

CHAPTER FIFTY

The team went down, hurtling through the void. The sensation of falling and the air rushing by was buffeting their suits. Feelings were but muted.

All of a sudden Wolf had a feeling, a very gut reaction that something was wrong. He stiffened and almost went into a spin.

"Hey is everybody all right, give me an okay if you are."

A large grunt was heard, then "Oh shit!"

"What's the matter, what's wrong?"

"I'm getting a reading, my chute is going to deploy in about thirty seconds," yelled Richard. "This is the perfect chute."

"If that happens, your drop zone will be off."

"Yes Wolf, Natalie broke in by approximately forty-nine and a half miles. Give or take five hundred yards."

Susie gasped, "So what happens to the chute, will it be ripped apart?"

"Jesus Sue, thanks for the help. The chute isn't opening yet but I've got about fifteen seconds."

"Is everything else okay – no damage to air flow, masks, your body?"

"Everything is fine, Wolf, but I'm going down and the chute just deployed."

Rich was suddenly stopped in mid-air. The chute had opened, but did not tear.

"It didn't tear, it held together, I guess it's stronger than it looks. I am drifting away, I am moving southwest slanting slowly down but definitely angling away from the immediate drop zone."

"Just like you, Rich, to leave the party just when the fun is going to start."

"Thanks Al, fuck you too."

"Gentlemen, if I may interject?"

"Of course you can Natalie, we're only falling faster than hell into a black void with no landmarks, trying to save the world from a terrible disease and having a goddamn surreal conversation though our minds while falling, but what the hell, interject."

"Yes Al, you're quite right and as far as the reading go, everyone except of course Rich, is on a correct path to land roughly one thousand feet from the mine entrance. Rich is moving further away and we'll son lose contact. Don't worry Rich, we'll get you."

"Thanks for the kind words, I'll . . . "

"He's out of range. He's gone." Silence filled the air. Shadow Team was out one man, and they hadn't even landed, yet.

CHAPTER FIFTY-ONE

There was one minute of free fall left when Natalie came into their minds. First a warm calming effect filtered though, then her thoughts blending with theirs, causing immediate calm although before the intrusion, they felt anything but.

The thoughts were directions on landing. Each member was going to be given separate instructions on how to land when their chutes deployed. Fifteen seconds to go, then the chutes opened, jerked the bodies up, then settled down. Natalie spoke to them. Wolf's guide lines were pulled one way, Al's another. Susie's and Mac's altogether different.

With thirty seconds to land, Natalie focused a narrow laser like beam of light to the ground resembling a red circle of about thirty feet circumference. This was to be their landing zone. With legs together and proper control of static lines, the chutes were coming down perfectly. The lift was there so the team would come in standing up with a slight reflex of legs to be able to walk away, and collapsing the chutes immediately.

Al landed first, stumbled a little. Grabbed the lines, dug in, collapsed the chute.

"Atta a baby, just go down," Mac grabbed his chute and was folding it. Mac landed with a little run, but came to a stop, collapsed the chute, and brought it quickly into his chest.

Wolf landed perfectly, having gone through some jump training before. Like a bicycle, once done never forgotten.

"Besides, Natalie's instructions were so good, even a baby could land."

No soon had Wolf spoken these words than a thump was heard, a loud "SNAP" and "Fucking son of a bitch. Help me guys, I broke my ankle."

CHAPTER FIFTY-TWO

"Susie, Susie, where are you?"

"Susie, you all right?"

"We're coming, just be calm."

"Gentlemen please, Susie is relatively safe. She is about twenty feet due east, I'm showing you where. She has a simple fracture. No displacement of bone. She'll be sidelined, but will be able to help you in a stationary way."

The men gathered around Susie.

"How ya doin' kid?"

"Hang in there."

"Don't move."

"Guys, guys, I'm all right except for the pain and the fact it's hard for me to walk."

"Mac, can you give her anything for the pain without affecting her mental facilities? We need her."

"As a matter of fact I can, Wolf, not to worry. I have here a pain inhibitor called ... are you ready? Vaxamine." Whereupon Mac moved his hands in a magician like way and held out a bottle of little green tablets.

"It's an all-natural botanical anti-inflammatory pain reliever that has proven to be as strong as any prescription drug but without any side effects. It is gastro and cardio friendly. Starts to work immediately and in about two hours, fifty percent of pain and inflammation is gone and she knows exactly what's going on."

"That's what we need. Susie, one of us was going to have to guard the mine entrance to Mattabassett. With your ankle, you're elected."

"Well thanks Wolf. It's good to know I'm appreciated, and not just any good looking, attractive female."

"Hey, we think you're that too Susie."

"Speak for yourself Al, I've always admired her brains," Mac smiled, making an outline of a jewel form.

"All right, all right, this is important. Susie, when we go in there … "

"Which will be in about ten minutes. Wolf, we do have a mission to complete and Susie's survival rate is approximately ninety-three point five percent if she stays out here. Of course, if the exit is breeched her survival rate … "

"Excuse me, Miss Natalie, but thanks for the info. Now listen Susie, if we don't make it, blow this opening. Hopefully we will have at least blown the other openings to keep them from getting out with vectors and virus."

"Rest assured Wolf, I will also be vigilant and make sure none escapes."

"So why are we going in then, if you're here and can stop them?"

"Because Al, there always has to be boots on the ground to make sure things get done."

"Great, as long as when we're done our boots are on out feet and not pointing up."

"Not to worry Al, Alpha will take care of you. Now shall we move Susie to her post?"

CHAPTER FIFTY-THREE

Natalie directed the group as Al and Mac aided Susie in walking.

"We landed fairly close to the mine opening. We should reach it ... ah, here it is."

On a slight incline and just in front of them, as the dawn started to emerge and light the rock face, was a black hole, dark and alone. No sounds, no signs of life. Abandoned two hundred and some years ago. The entrance to what had been people's dreams of success and riches, now could lead to a horrible, life ending nightmare.

"All right Susie, you stay here, you have enough water and energy tablets to last several days. If everything goes well, we should be back in thirty-two hours. If not, use those nitro sticks to blow this entrance. We won't be using it."

"Well I appreciate your trust and words of wisdom, since there's no place to go anyway. So I'll be back here. I don't have anywhere else to go."

"Don't worry Susie, I'll be with you all. If anything goes wrong, I'll let you know and you can act accordingly."

"Thank you so much Natalie, for those words of comfort. You just don't know how secure you've made me feel. I don't have a fear in the world knowing you're with me, your rod and your staff."

"Sarcasm ill befits one so young."

"Now gentlemen, shall we proceed?"

"Now I really do feel like I'm going into 'Dante's pit'. Hope we all come out of it."

"Don't worry Mac, 'Big Al' is here and our leader, and of course Natalie."

"Well Al, there's one thing I wanted to tell you before you entered."

"I sense an uh-oh coming, or at least a but."

"Right, well, for the period you are in this shaft you are on your own. I just found out there is some sort of influence that is going to keep me from communicating with you."

"You're kidding, all this bullshit and no commo, what the hell … "

"Easy big fella, calm down. What the hell, if everything went smoothly, we wouldn't have anything to brag about when we get out of here. We can live without Natalie for three quarters of a mile under tons of earth, ready to crush us. Right?"

"Wolf, I am so glad you have such a positive attitude. It just fills me with … "

"I know, I know, Mac. That's just my way. So guys, put on your neon lights and let's take a walk in the dark. Susie, take care. Natalie, we'll meet you at the other end."

The men turned on their helmet lights, made sure they had extra oxygen and cartridges, checked their weapons, and walked into the mine.

"Hey guys, by the way, did I ever tell you I was afraid of the dark?"

"Great."

"Shut up, Al."

CHAPTER FIFTY-FOUR

The three men walked along the dark mine shaft going deeper and deeper, and it was almost like HALO except they had their infra on and everything was clear. They walked around and climbed over some rocks. Any impediment so far wasn't.

"This is relatively simple, hey Wolf?"

"So far so good, but I wouldn't call it home."

They passed slabs of metal, rusted ore cars, and materials left there when the mine went bust. They rounded a corner. It stopped.

"Hey, what the hell is this?"

"Well Mac, I would say this is the end of the tunnel," spoke Al with a sarcastic tone, "It's all she wrote."

"Hold it, the map," as Wolf pulled out a flat surface pad, "We can go further, it's just a blockage. This tunnel goes all the way to Mattabassett."

"So what do we do? Use our blast sticks or lasers?"

"I would try our lasers, they're used for heavy cutting. That's what we need here, it's good for the lab so why not now. Okay guys, stand back I'll give it a try."

Wolf took out a small red stick which looked like a large cigar and aimed the stick at the wall right at the tip where the ceiling meets the tunnel. There was a crisp static like sound as the wall started to disintegrate.

"I'll cut a large enough hole and then we'll go through. I don't know how secure this wall is but it might shift with pressure released from cutting and we could be in deep shit."

The hole became bigger with no apparent problem. It was now about three feet from the ground. Wolf stopped.

"Okay, climb through carefully and quickly. This will probably hold, but we don't know."

Al was already through before Wolf had stopped cutting. Mac had grabbed Al's hand and was going through. All of a sudden little pebbles started to fall, then bigger ones.

"Shit." Wolf looked around, saw a fairly large piece of sheet metal, "Here, grab this, put it up, make it a ceiling – your suits are on full so you should be able to handle the pressure."

Mac and Al pushed up the sheet. Wolf took two steps back, ran and jumped through. The steel sheeting cut loose, fell, taking a little bit of his boot heel off.

"Thanks guys. Appreciate it, I owe you."

"No problem, how many times in one's life does he act like a ceiling beam?"

"Yeah Al, I sort of felt like Atlas myself."

They moved on.

CHAPTER FIFTY-FIVE

They continued their walk through the tunnel.

"We should be getting closer, shouldn't we Wolf."

"Al, we're about maybe a quarter of a mile before we hit the Mattabassett wall."

"So those laser sticks should work and get us through, right?"

"They'll work, all right. When Natalie feels the heat on the wall, she'll short circuit any alarm system that would go off letting them know we're here."

"So what's the story, the head of this installation sold out to her lover, then they're going to escape by chopper and blackmail the world?"

"Right, screwy as it sounds, we are here to stop them. These two are killers and traitors but not professionals. So in a way, it's easier to get to them, than say a professional thief or assassin whose thought process and emotions are under control. These women should be easier to get to."

"So Wolf, we cut a hole, go in, find them and what? Kill them?"

"No, no Mac."

"These two once we face them should be easy. We have our suits, Natalie, and weapons. There's no problem that I can see. They have no suicidal motives ..."

"As far as we know Wolf, but they could be nuttier than a fruit cake."

"They could, Al, but that's what we get the big bucks for, going out and getting the bad guys."

They continued along the tunnel until …

"Hey, what's that?"

"Looks like an opening."

"Great, we need a hole like we need Swiss cheese."

Wolf and Mac looked at Al. "Okay so it's not funny, but it sounded good in my mind."

"Yeah right, next time keep it."

"What ya want, I'm under a lot of stress."

"Mac, Al, this opening is about twelve feet across. With our suits, we should be able to jump this with no trouble."

"Yeah, no trouble. Well Wolf you're the leader, you go first."

"Right, I'll go first then Mac, then Al. Make sure to jump more than less."

"You're kidding, I'm gonna jump short so I can see how deep the hole is?"

"Cut the crap, let's go."

Wolf took a couple of steps back, took a run and jumped. He landed about five feet after the hole.

"No problem, just concentrate on pushing your muscles, run then jump."

"Ok, here I come," Mac took a couple of steps, turned quickly, ran, jumped – Wolf grabbed his arm.

"Safe."

"Told you. Okay Al, jump."

Al moved back, started to jump, then stopped, turned around, walked back, and then looked at them.

"I'm afraid. I can't do it."

"You just jumped out of a plane for Christ's sake, what do you mean afraid? We have a job to do, let's go, cut the bullshit."

"All right, all right."

"I can do it, I can do it."

Al was a sweat rag. He was scared. He pushed off with his hands from the wall, took four running steps and jumped. He looked straight at Wolf's eyes, he felt Wolf's hand grab his arm, Mac the other. They pulled back, fell on top of each other.

"Rough landing guys, but one we can walk away from."

They got up and dusted themselves off and started walking and turned a corner. There it was, the roughhewn rock wall of Mattabassett.

CHAPTER FIFTY-SIX

"Right, this is a wall but how do we know this is the right wall? It looks like a mine wall to me, no different than the rest."

"You're absolutely correct, Al my friend, but if you'll both step back we'll find out real quick."

"What are you going to do Wolf, press your magic wand and bingo it's the one?"

"Right Mac, watch."

Wolf took out his laser stick. Pushed a couple of buttons, aimed it at the wall. A light pulsed out. Wolf moved his wand in a small circle of about two feet in diameter. The black wall started to dissolve before their eyes. The hole grew deeper. Wolf stopped, looked into the opening. Not satisfied, he pushed the button again. Once again the light pulsed and more wall disappeared, finally a little buzz sounded, then became louder. Wolf stopped. He put his hand into the opening and brushed the surface. A metal surface could be seen. He brushed more. The metal wall shone through.

"Well boys, that's the Wall."

"We hit pay dirt, or wall if you will," joked Al.

"Now stand back, I'm going to put this baby on full. In a few minutes we should be in Mattabassett."

The light pulsed, stronger this time, more of the mine wall was vaporized, the opening grew. Finally after about five minutes, a steel like surface could be seen. This time it was about six feet high and four feet wide. Wolf made a few more adjustments, aimed it at the steel surface. At first nothing happened, then the steel started to move, shimmer. The opening grew higher and bigger. No smoke, nothing, the wall disappeared. Light started to appear as the opening grew bigger. Finally the hole was a doorway. A hallway could be seen. They had broken though.

"Man, that's about three feet deep and you cut through it like a hot scoop through ice cream."

"Basically Mac, not far from wrong. The wand puts out such a strong beam that the molecules that are the wall dissolve so quickly that anyone standing on the other side doesn't even know the wall has been breached."

They entered the hole. All of a sudden Natalie's voice came through.

"I see you have gotten in. Unfortunately I can't be with you. The same material that prevented me from guiding you through the shaft is in Mattabassett."

"So how are you talking to us now?"

"When you blasted through the wall, whatever interference has been interrupted."

"Great, so we're blind again. Anything else you care to let us in on?"

"Yes. Point of fact, the good news is that through this hole I have been able to disarm the main alarm system so you can walk in fairly safely. The bad news is there still may be small alarms and traps that could be set off. They run independently of the main system."

The men stepped into the corridor. They looked around.

Wolf went back into the hole.

"Which way do we go?"

"You go to the left, that's where the main lab is. There are elevators. Go down two levels. The two women are in a lounge area, waiting for a signal from above telling them their ride is here. It will never come. They don't know that. They have a small receiver that will beep when their ride comes."

"So how come you can't breach that receiver and worm your way through to the main console?"

"I have been trying, Mac, but to no avail."

"You are on your own, Wolf. You and your team, you've come this far, no reason not to go on."

"It'll be a walk in the park. No problem."

"You'll have problems and it won't be a walk in the park, but you can do it."

CHAPTER FIFTY-SEVEN

They cautiously walked down the corridor, looking left and right as they passed closed doors. Some bodies were lying around in various poses – none had died easy.

"According to Natalie before we were cut off, there are traps that are set off if the right sequence isn't given."

"But Wolf, she turned everything off when we went through the wall. We can't communicate, but evidently that breach made it possible for her to control everything."

"If that's true, Mac, then this should be a walk in the park. We'll still practice due diligence, just to make sure. These people are not contagious, but be careful."

"No problem guys, I'm in no hurry to go to heaven."

"Right Al, that's where you'll go all right."

"Now, now Mac, don't be jealous."

As they walked to the elevator, which would take them down to the safe room, Rich, twenty miles away, was just waking up.

"Son of a bitch, I'm alive," he groaned, slowly rolling over and looking up at the stars. He felt his body. Carefully moving arms and legs, lifting his head.

"Thank you, Jesus. I don't know how, but I'm alive and nothing's broke."

He looked at this compass which he recovered from one of the pockets on the suit. A steady light flashed at basically an Eastern direction.

"Well, that's where they are. I'm here, so I better get going. Natalie, Natalie, are you there?"

No answer came from the darkness. Just the eternal blinking of the stars alone.

"Well Rich me boy, you've got a little walk ahead of you, so let's go."

He slowly picked himself up, drank water from his reserve, and started off towards the blinking light, his infra system lighting the way.

CHAPTER FIFTY-EIGHT

At Mattabassett, the men had reached the elevator leading down to the safe room.

"With all these bodies around, it looks like it hit pretty fast."

"I don't know Al, supposedly they let the virus go and beat feet to the safe room, locking themselves in until the all clear."

"Natalie disabled the all clear sign. That's why they're still there. Too scared to leave."

"This virus kills, Wolf, but maybe they thought down here it's such a sterile environment it wouldn't disperse as fast. Maybe the people could get themselves to the infirmary or other safe room before they died."

"Could be, right now we get to the ladies. Don't shoot unless you have to. We want them alive. They have to answer a lot of questions."

"Right Boss," Al saluted, "We will take them alive or die trying."

Wolf pushed the button for the alarm, touched the numeric code on the pad. A moment later a little "ding" was heard. The elevator had arrived. They got in, Wolf pushed a dial marked three, and down they went. Another "ding" and the door opened. They stepped out.

"The safe room should be this way."

Wolf walked to the right, down to a door on the left, painted lime green. They saw the door opening and closing with a soft thud. Wolf motioned with his hand. Al to stop, Mac to the right. He continued. They hugged the wall, listening to the soft thud, thud of the door trying to close. Wolf motioned, he would go in first, hold the door, then Mac, then Al would go in.

He raised his hand, put three fingers up. Al and Mac nodded.

One finger went up. He moved. He held the door open, Mac and Al went in left and right. Wolf followed.

Straight in front of them was Carol and Karen sitting side by side, dried blood on their faces, skin bluish gray.

"Don't touch anything, guys. No chance. They're dead, the virus got them."

Mac motioned to the door, "When they came in here, one of them dropped a pen. It got stick in the track and the door wouldn't close."

The men moved out of the room.

"We'll go back, tell Natalie what we found. She can tell us how to leave and also get a cleanup crew in here and do what they have to do."

The men walked back, made contact with Natalie. Directions were given, up they went breathing a sigh of relief. They went through two safety doors and a containment room where they could manually sterilize themselves. One last door and they were out.

They sun was out. The sky was blue. Sue waved to them and they walked over and hugged. Wolf made contact with Natalie. Biernacki and LaCoste would be there shortly.

Wolf looked to the West and saw a figure in the horizon.

"Well I'll be." The rest looked. The figure drew closer.

Rich waved.

They moved towards him.

"Nice of you to join us."

"A little late, I see."

"Hey, better late than never."

"Okay guys, let's sit down in the shade and we can tell war stories. Biernacki and LaCoste will be picking us up soon and then back to Alpha."

Epilogue

Two days had passed since the team returned from their mission. They were going to conference room three for their final briefing to wrap up the incident at Mattabassett.

As soon as they walked into conference room three, they knew something was up.

Wolf looked around. The room was large with a huge oval table in the middle. Lighting was low, several bouquets of flowers on polished tables. Oil paintings by some very famous, if not dead, artists and a very homey atmosphere pervaded his senses. He recognized Natalie's touch, probably so did the rest of the team.

At the table, already seated, were Malcolm Fletcher, Biernacki and LaCoste, Barbara, Grafton, Julius, Josiah, and Frank. He was surprised.

They stood and clapped as the Shadow Team walked into the room.

Frank spoke, "Welcome Shadow Team, you have completed your tests and are now members of Alpha. Please be seated."

The team looked at each other as they sat. Wondering what test. What was going on.

"Excuse me Frank, but what test? We just came off a mission."

"Yeah," chimed in Al, "and saved the world from certain death."

"Yes, quite right, Mr. Al, but almost, not exactly," smiled Grafton. "Maybe if I explained the situation, it would be easier to understand."

The group turned to a woman who was seated at the curve of the table.

Wolf noticed the lighting pulsed slightly.

"No way," he said aloud. He nudged Sue, who raised her eyebrow and hit Al, who passed it along to Mac, then Rich.

"Ah, Mr. Wolf, a very astute observer. The woman appeared to be about fifty years old, black hair, hugged close to her face in a straight style. Her face was oval, skin olive complexion with a hint of rouge and pink lipstick. She had a nice smile. She wore a white blouse open at the neck. As she got up and walked to a slightly higher platform, her height, now about five feet seven and a quarter. Good figure.

"I am, if you have not already guessed, Natalie, in a perfect as can be made virtual model. We felt you needed a realistic model to keep in touch with, and this is it."

"Now ladies and gentlemen, and Shadow Team members. The assignment you were on was a test from the very beginning. Everything was rigged, from Barbra, to the virus, the breaching of the mine, to the bodies all around you."

"But they were real, I know they were!" exclaimed Mac.

"Do you mean like this?" In a flash, on the table were three bodies in grotesque posters, with the smell of death exploding from them. The smell disappeared as quickly as it had come, but the bodies remained.

"Touch them, feel them, see what they are."

Rich reached out, along with Al and the rest of the team, expecting flesh and bone, but knowing how could they be real since they just appeared.

Wolf put out his hand, touched the body – nothing – just air. He moved his hand around – nothing. They were there, but they weren't.

Everyone was amazed, stunned.

"What the hell is going on?"

"What is going on, Al, is that you are looking at the best virtual reality imagining that exists."

The bodies vanished.

"You'll remember, Wolf, you were told not to touch the bodies or anything around, with the exception of walls, doors. That was to make sure the illusion would not be broken. However, if you did touch something, I put in your mind the feeling of that touch, and smell."

"Okay, so the mission was a test, but what about the mine, Susie's ankle, Rich falling? Tests?"

"Not quite. That was the small percentage I gave you all for the failure of the mission."

"The way you handled those misadventures, however, made the mission a complete success."

"So going back a little, even the ladies were pretend?"

"Yes Susie, they were a pretend story to get you people worked up."

"As I stated before, you all behaved beautifully." She smiled. "Shadow Team, Welcome to Alpha."

With that, Natalie disappeared.

Grafton welcomed all to Alpha. Waiters came in with trays of food, low music played, and everyone enjoyed themselves.

Wolf woke up the next morning to the sound of his phone ringing.

"This is Fletcher. Mr. Wolf, at 1100 hours, Biernacki and Captain LaCoste will be picking you up and taking you to see a Doctor Jeffrey Wilder."

"Okay, why?"

"Why? Why? For a new mission, Mr. Wolf, that's why."

13319477R00133

Made in the USA
Charleston, SC
01 July 2012